Ju
F
N93
b

Nurenberg, Thelma.
The time of anger.

𝕿𝖊𝖒𝖕𝖑𝖊 𝕴𝖘𝖗𝖆𝖊𝖑

𝕷𝖎𝖇𝖗𝖆𝖗𝖞

Minneapolis, Minn.

———

Please sign your full name on the above card.

Return books promptly to the Library or Temple Office.

Fines will be charged for overdue books or for damage or loss of same.

THE TIME OF ANGER

THE TIME OF ANGER

by Thelma Nurenberg

Abelard-Schuman
New York

Books by Thelma Nurenberg

My Cousin, the Arab
The Time of Anger

Library of Congress Cataloging in Publication Data

Nurenberg, Thelma.
     The time of anger.
     Summary: The slowly developing friendship between
the young people of a kibbutz and a nearby Arab village
is threatened by the outbreak of the Six-Day War of 1967.
     [1. Israel-Arab War, 1967—Fiction] I. Title.
PZ7.N965Ti   [Fic]   75-2396
ISBN 0-200-00153-1

10   9   8   7   6   5   4   3   2   1

To Irving Warshaw,
for goodness remembered

Glossary

abayah (Arab.) Arab cloak
abba (Hebrew) father
Ah'lan wasaha 'ilan (Arab.) you are welcome
Al Fatiha (Arab.) Moslem prayer
aluf (Hebrew) major general in the Israeli army
beseder (Hebrew) okay, all right
bimbashi (Turk.) police chief during the Ottoman regime
boker tov (Hebrew) good morning
bride-price dowry the bridegroom gives to family of bride
caftan (Hebrew) a long, coatlike garment with a sash at the waist
chaverim (Hebrew) comrades
Chazak v'amots (Hebrew) with strength and courage
cheinik (Hebrew) teakettle
debka (Arab.) Arab dance
diwan (Arab.) guest house
dunim (Hebrew) one-quarter of an acre
effendi (Arab.) title of respect
El Mahleh Rahamin (Hebrew) God is full of mercy
fedayeen (Arab.) Arab terrorists
fellaheen (Arab.) Arab peasants
fez (Arab.) a small, round cap with a tassel worn by men in the
    Middle East
Hamdu 'Illah (Arab.) Praise be to Allah
hamula (Arab.) a clan or a group of related families
hora (Hebrew) Israeli round dance
ima (Hebrew) mother
Inshallah (Arab.) if Allah wills
kheffiyah (Arab.) broad scarf used as a headdress
kibbutz (Hebrew) collective agricultural settlement
kibbutzim (Hebrew) plural of *kibbutz*
kiddush (Hebrew) prayer over wine and over bread
Knesset (Hebrew) parliament
kumsitz (Hebrew) a small tea party
leben (Arab.) yogurt
Ma'a Salameh (Arab.) Go in peace
mazel tov (Hebrew) good luck
mizmar (Arab.) double reed pipe. Any wind instrument

mosque (Arab.) a Moslem place of worship

mukhtar (Arab.) the head or mayor of an Arab village

mullah (Arab.) a Moslem teacher, expounder of the Koran

nargileh (Arab.) water jar with pipe for tobacco smoking

nu (Hebrew) (an expression) "so?"

Passover (Hebrew) Festival of Freedom commemorating the Hebrews' liberation by Moses from bondage in Egypt, and the Exodus

pitta (Arab.) flat, round bread

purdah (Arab.) long black veil covering a woman's face and body

Purim (Hebrew) festival commemorating deliverance of the Jews in Persia from execution by Haman

rabbi (Hebrew) a Jewish minister or teacher

sabba (Hebrew) grandfather

Sabbath (Hebrew) Saturday. Jewish Sabbath is from sundown on Friday until sundown on Saturday

scimitar (Oriental) a curved sword

seder (Hebrew) first two evening meals at Passover

shabbat (Hebrew) the Jewish Sabbath

shaitan (Arab.) devil

shalom (Hebrew) peace. Also used in greeting or farewell

sheket (Hebrew) be quiet

shofar (Hebrew) a ram's horn

sura (Arab.) a section or chapter in the Koran

tov (Hebrew) good

vattik (Hebrew) a veteran or one of the founders of a *kibbutz*

wadi (Arab.) dry river bed

Yom Kippur (Hebrew) holiest day in the Jewish year; a day of prayer and fasting

zmira (Hebrew) table hymns sung at the end of the Sabbath and holiday meals

～ Contents

THE TIME OF ANGER

1

A Daring Student Project
in the *Kibbutz*

It was late February and, after the heavy rains, the orchards were sun-drenched and sweetly fragrant with blossoms that spread over the fruit trees like frothy white clouds. But the girl climbing the long steep hill of Kibbutz Tel Hashava to its old military field was, for once, unaware of the beauty that surrounded her.

Being young wasn't the joy that the old ones said it was, Aviva thought. Whether or not they willed it, you inherited their problems and created some of your own.

And it was not true that life is what your thoughts make it. That is escapism. War is a fact of life and your thoughts can't make it anything else! It has to be confronted realistically.

Reaching the summit of the field, she stood a

moment, caught by the awesome grandeur of the Syrian escarpment in the distance that blended into the sky. Against the vast sweep of those craggy bluffs, Amitai—the *kibbutz* cowboy—and his horse looked toy-sized as they galloped across the pasture to the far border fence to round up his precious strays.

Here all was so serene and innocent that Aviva found it impossible to believe that the heaps of rocks and the scattering of stone houses on the Syrian hills concealed the artillery that last month shelled their neighboring *kibbutz*.

What was it like for the young in other countries who did not inherit wars and troubles? In America her father had told her, the seventeen-to-eighteen-year-olds were ready for the university, or a technical school, or some kind of work or—like herself—to study the performing arts.

In Israel you had to go into the army. All your growing years you were pampered with love and then you had to learn to kill.

Aviva thought about all this as she walked about the field, idly picking wildflowers, and then sat down on a boulder. The letter from her American father slipped out of her pocket, and she shoved it back in. She had already read it twice: He wanted her to live with him in New York; he had already inquired at the High School of Performing Arts about enrolling her, and her grades made her eligible. He wanted her to come at once as war was inevitable.

Nearby, the rusty barrel of a disused cannon peeped out of the tall weeds, and she thought that if only all the guns across the Arab borders were as rusty from disuse, she'd have no problems.

The fear that had seized her earlier, when she had tuned in on Cairo, had subsided, but from that fear, to her surprise, she had learned a basic truth about herself—she was a coward and not to be relied on in a time of crisis.

She took out the letter from her pocket again. Should she go to New York?

If she went, would Erni forget her? Would he marry while she was away? Would the kids at the *kibbutz* think her a deserter?

What should she write her father . . . ?

"Aviva!"

Yoram stood before her. Moshe was with him, the last few notes from his harmonica lingering softly in the air. She had been concentrating so fiercely on a decision that she hadn't heard them approaching.

"What are you doing up here when you're needed below?" Yoram demanded. Aviva looked at him coldly. Since he had become the leader of the secondary school seniors, he neither asked nor requested anything. He demanded. He was practicing to behave like the officer he hoped to be when he went into the army on his eighteenth birthday. He was stocky and muscular, and now sweat beaded his blunt nose and ran from his brush-short hair down his square-shaped, fleshy face.

Tapping the moisture out of his harmonica, Moshe grinned at her sheepishly. With his dark messy hair, his bulging eyes blinking behind thick spectacles, his gargoyle face looked so idiotically guilty that, despite her anger, she laughed.

He must have seen her slip away, after the voting on the Umm Tubas Work-Study Project, when the kids went to the dining hall for their snacks. He had brought Yoram here, clearly a breach of friendship, for even though Moshe was only sixteen, he was her closest friend and, as a composer and fellow artist, he knew her occasional need for solitude. She would deal with him later, and now she dismissed him with a withering look.

"What's the problem?" she snapped at Yoram.

"The general meeting tomorrow night," Yoram replied. "We've not much time to convince them."

"Would our talking to the old ones matter? They're worried over more crucial things," she said.

What had gotten into her that suddenly made her so contrary? Yoram wondered. When Aviva's mother, Ora, first proposed that a group of Israeli Arab youths from Umm Tubas, their neighboring village, come to live, study and work in the *kibbutz* for one year, Aviva had worked passionately to win support for the project. Today, the secondary school had voted almost unanimously for it—but it had yet to be approved by the *kibbutz* members.

Yoram bristled. "Listen, Vivi, we don't know if there will be war or not, but we must act as if we've a future and plan ahead. Ora said this."

Yes, her mother had said this but somehow it hadn't allayed her fears, and Aviva wondered about this because Ora was usually so convincing.

Moshe did not feel offended that Aviva was angry with him, but why was she so moody when she had to convince the old ones, particularly Amitai and his bunch, into voting for the Arab Work-Study Project? Hadn't she said that getting the old ones to accept it would be a test of student power?

Finally, he said, "Vivi, if you can't talk them into voting yes, no one can."

Rising, she brushed bits of earth from the back of her shorts and said edgily, "You can't blame Amitai—or the others—for being against the project. That mine the terrorist planted last month nearly killed Noah—all the cows they stole—all those threats and . . ." She saw Yoram's jaws clench with challenge, saw Moshe's reproachful look, and added: "Besides, there may not even be a meeting tomorrow night."

"Why not?" Yoram asked.

"Well, you know how sick Abu Sa'id is. If he dies . . ."

"What has that to do with the meeting?"

"Well, Abu Sa'id is our friend; what he says is law in Umm Tubas. That's why there are such good relations between our villages."

"If good relations between us depend on only one man, it is not a healthy situation," Moshe remarked.

Gathering the field flowers scattered at her feet, Aviva thought that Moshe, a mediocre student whom she often had to coach, said very wise things at times.

Yoram said, "Abu Sa'id is a tough old bird, and Dr. Erni thinks he may recover. And we've got to tackle the old ones."

She heard the clink of stone on stone and looked around. There was movement in the tall weeds and a shaggy head of silvery-gold hair emerged. Adam! Ugh, she grimaced. In the year since he had come from Poland, he had succeeded in making himself the most unpopular young male in the *kibbutz.* He had disdained her efforts at friendship, as well as her offer to help him with his Hebrew. It had been the first time she had ever been rejected, and it still rankled.

He came through the weeds, zigzagging as he kicked one stone at another and, in his shorts, his long thin legs made him look like a stork. He had a long, flat, high-cheeked face with a short up-turned nose, and his eyes were such a bright blue you forgot how homely he really was. He wore a heavy gray sweater that still bore the letter of the sports club of his school in Poland.

Yoram saw him and grumbled, "Him!"

"Remember what Ora said yesterday," Aviva said warningly. "You can do more with sugar than with vinegar."

"Right now we're short of sugar," Yoram said. It was Moshe who called out, "*Shalom,* Adam." Aviva waved him over. Adam continued kicking one stone with the other, but now in their direction. A concession!

"Adam, we're talking about the Arab Work-Study Project," Yoram said, the affable class leader now. "We've got a list of those we must talk to before the general meeting. Want to tackle one of them?"

Adam picked up the two round stones and dexterously juggled them high in the air. Then, catching them, one in each hand, he said in English: "That's your problem," and walked away.

Outraged, they glared at him until he was out of sight.

With a sigh Moshe said, "He doesn't ask for his mail anymore. His mother never writes. Even his father stopped coming from Jerusalem for the *Shabbat*. It is very sad for him."

"There are worse things happening here," Yoram said. "He's been here a whole year and still refuses to speak Hebrew, only Polish or English. Last night he kept the light on in our room very late. He'd brought a map of Europe from the library, and was measuring the land miles from here to Poland. I asked him what for, and he said that one day he'd walk back home. I told him he wasn't wanted in Poland and . . ."

"Yoram! That was a brutal thing to say!" Aviva exclaimed.

"The way he treats us—he doesn't deserve Israel!" Yoram retorted.

"That's not for you to say!" Moshe whipped back.

Aviva began tying the flowers together with a weed. Yoram caught the dejected look on her face as she turned to leave. "Vivi, anything wrong?"

She flushed. Never before had he been sensitive to her moods. "Why do you ask?"

"You look, well, sort of, like something's bothering you."

"I didn't know you had such an imagination. Of course I'll work on Amitai and the old bunch," and, with a lift of her chin, she flounced past him to the hill road. Moshe watched her graceful, swinging stride and then plunged after her, piping "The Bridge on the River Kwai" on his harmonica.

The tune rippled across the air like the gay warblings of birds, on this first sun-filled spring morning after the heavy rains, and Aviva quickened to its rhythm. It made her feel like dancing, but she resisted the impulse. She was still angry with Moshe and Yoram for invading her privacy. She had come up here to work on a decision and was returning with her problem unsolved.

In the Arab-Israeli village of Umm Tubas, Fared had not yet come when Laila Tabari reached the Tomb of the Holy Man. She was early, but she had hoped to find him waiting for her. They hadn't seen each other in the month since she had graduated from the secondary school in Nazareth.

Branches of the gnarled old olive tree hung low over the dome of the tomb, with bits of paper, inscribed with prayers to Allah, stuck onto the twigs. Laila had written one for her neighbor, Fatma, an illiterate woman. Fatma had dictated:

I pray, O Allah, for the health of Abu Sa'id el Khoury, the father of Khalil, whose son is Fared. I pray, O Allah, for the health of my husband Ibrahim, who is sick from the heavy rains so now I pull the plow.

Your faithful servant,
Fatma in Umm Tubas

A few branches were tied about with small rags, left there by women who could not write, and did not have neighbors who could. They hoped that the holy man buried in the tomb would know their needs and intercede for them.

Fared was sure to come from the main street, and Laila climbed the steep hill to watch for him. Below, on a rise in the land, was the mosque whose gold dome and graceful minaret could be seen throughout Umm Tubas. Nestled against it was the Moslem religious school which Fared had attended until his thirteenth year and where, he told her, the *Mullah* had tried to knock the Koran into his head with a knobby stick.

To the west lay the hilly fields of Kibbutz Tel Hashava, with the walls of two buildings shimmering white in the glare of the sun, and gray where it stood in the shadows cast by the steep cliffs of the Syrian escarpment.

Would there be war? Laila wondered.

Fared should have been here by now. Why was he late?

Her father had already given his consent that she enroll in the *kibbutz* work-study program, but her three brothers were not as optimistic as he was: Nightly they tuned in on the Cairo and Damascus radio stations, and nightly the announcements grew more threatening—Israel was doomed! Her mother was nervous at the prospect of her going; the *kibbutz* stood directly in the line of Syrian fire, but her father dismissed her mother's fears. He said, "The Arab armies tried to crush Israel in '48, tried again in '55 and now, in 1967, they surely can't."

Waiting, Laila questioned her motive. Why did she want to join the work-study group? To learn about *kibbutzim?* No, the bald and shaming truth was, she admitted to herself, because of Fared.

She was secretly betrothed to him and wore the ring he had given her on a string under her blouse. It was a secret of which she was ashamed; her parents did not deserve this of her. But until Fared's grandfather, Abu Sa'id el Khoury, approached her father with a marriage offer, she and Fared had to keep their love a secret.

And now Fared's grandfather, whom he adored, was very ill. Their situation was further complicated by the fact that her father did not belong to any *hamula* and was thus without social status, while Fared's people were wealthy and had great prestige throughout the area. She was certain that the grandfather, a wise and venerable man, would overlook the matter of the *hamula,* but Fared's father was status- and money-minded.

She knew Fared's faults: He was fickle and quite vain, had been a lazy, indifferent student in secondary school, and probably loved the red sports car his father had given him last month, at his graduation, more than he loved her.

Although they had gone to separate schools in Nazareth, they had managed to see each other quite often. But here, in Umm Tubas, a Moslem girl does not make dates with a male. In the *kibbutz,* however, she might see him daily.

Fared was late again. She had no watch, but she felt the lateness. He would come and, without an apology, plunge into whatever was on his mind and never admit to being late. Had his grandfather's condition worsened? She shuddered at the thought. The villagers always turned to Abu Sa'id for counsel —and help.

She marveled that Fared had chosen her when many girls of his *hamula* were beautiful. She knew that she was very plain-looking, with a long face and even a longish nose. But Fared said often enough—

and she chose to believe him—that her eyes, the bright blue of a cornflower, were very expressive, and gave her an interesting sort of beauty that all the other girls lacked. Once he said, "You're always so serious, but when you smile, your face lights up and is positively beautiful!"

It was surprising how well they got along together, because she had taken her studies seriously while he hadn't. Mainly, they talked about soccer, or about his favorite sport, basketball. Sometimes she managed to bring their talk to a social or political problem and, after his first flippant remark, he would express a serious thought. She felt certain that he was only a lazy thinker, who had to be prodded for his intelligence to surface. He was quite unpredictable, but she felt deeply that his love for her was unwavering.

If they went to the *kibbutz* . . . She gave a start, feeling his approach even before she heard the sound of his steps over broken twigs. She waited for him to reach her.

Tall and slender, Fared moved with supple grace, and she thrilled at how handsome and masculine he was. She liked the fact that he was always neatly dressed when he met her, and did not affect an air of careless abandon as did his friend Abdul, whose sloppy appearance, particularly his hair, made him look as wild and defiant as he sounded. Fared's hair was shiny black, combed neatly into waves, and was always scented with pomade.

As he climbed, he looked up and smiled, and she laughed a little giddily that he had come at last.

Fared loped the remaining distance between

them and seized her in his arms. "You are late!" he scolded, with that teasing smile that always melted whatever anger was in her. He had a habit of faulting her for being only a minute late while he was rarely on time—and he had a wristwatch! She held his face between her hands. His eyes were lustrous, a soft velvety brown, and his slightly beaked, firm-boned nose gave strength to his swarthy long face with its full-fleshed, pliant mouth. She kissed him and drew away, asking, "How is your grandfather?"

"*Hamdu 'Illah!*" he said, as he removed his tweed jacket and spread it over the ground—still damp from the recent heavy rains. Then he settled her on it and sat down beside her, his long legs against hers. Demurely, she pulled the skirt of her brown dress below her knees.

He plucked a fragment of leaf from her hair, which she wore in braids down her back, saying as he did so, "Dr. Erni told us my grandfather has an iron grip on life. But last week my father had to phone the *kibbutz* in the middle of the night for Dr. Erni to come. I've cut two games. I can't play when he's so sick."

In commiseration she pressed her cheek against his and murmured, "He'll live. He's got to! The village can't do without him."

"I would have been here earlier, waiting for you, but Abdul came with a gift from his grandfather to mine."

She frowned but said nothing. She detested Abdul and did not know whether it was because she was jealous of their close friendship or because he had influence over Fared, which she considered harmful. Adnan, her youngest brother, who went to their school, said that Abdul was a disruptive force among the students.

Quietly, she said, "Fared, someone scribbled 'Nasser' on the walls of the Dress Cooperative and Clinic. Who does this? Abdul?"

Instantly, his face tightened. "I don't keep in his shadow, so I don't know," he said dryly.

She felt him withdrawing from her. His arm dropped from her shoulder, and he held himself stiffly aloof. With her words, she had changed his mood from love to hostility. It was always like this when she said something critical of Abdul. And, with a wrench at her heart, she thought that if the measure of his love was determined by her attitude to Abdul, then their relationship had better end right now! She stirred to get up.

"Don't go, Laila," he said with sudden urgency, gripping her arm. "To hell with Abdul! He's not worth a quarrel," and he hugged her, frightened that he had already lost her.

Then he said, "I'm late because old Noah, Dr. Erni and Ora came to see my grandfather."

She smiled. "Did Ora say anything about the work-study project?" she asked.

"Not this morning, but the other day she said that the *kibbutz* members had still to vote on it."

"Fared, why will you enroll?"

"My grandfather wants me to," he said and shrugged, frowning into space. "I guess it's as good a way as any to kill time until I take my entrance exams at Hebrew University. Anyway, it will improve my Hebrew and it needs improving."

At least he was honest, but she felt humbled. She had hoped he would say "because you are going." And then she heard him add, "And you will be there!"

"Oh, I'm so glad!" she cried, her face bright with joy.

"How else will I see you? Of course it will be interesting up there—they've a good soccer team and their sports field is first-rate. And I really need the Hebrew."

"So do I! I'm so nervous at the thought of that entrance exam. I was told Hebrew University exams are the stiffest anywhere."

"You had the highest grades—and you worry?" His voice went high with disbelief.

"Over Hebrew, yes. I'd like to see what it's like in the *kibbutz*. It would be almost like going to a foreign country," she said.

"I'm told they've enough foreigners there to make it foreign," he added, and they both laughed.

Thoughtfully she began plucking at the grass and then said nervously, "Maybe the *kibbutz* members will reject the project."

"I doubt it. Ora and old Noah are all for it—and they carry a lot of weight."

She nodded, but felt uncertain. She rose and said wistfully, "Fared, don't go down with me. There are a few women at the tomb."

Embracing her, he said, "Tell Adnan I'll visit this week," and they smiled at this shared conspiracy. He had come several times to visit Adnan and, while he chatted with her father and brothers, he never once directed a glance at the far side of the room, where she sat reading. Yet both felt they had been together.

2

Fared Joins the Work-Study Group

That February of 1967, the rains came down heavily, saturating the Galilee Hills, so that the *fellaheen* of Umm Tubas found the plowing less burdensome than usual. In past seasons they worked with hope easing their efforts—a good crop—surely! And if the sun failed to spark the seeds into life, there was always the Old Warrior, Abu Sa'id el Khoury, who saw to it that no one starved.

But now, even with the rains that augured well, they worked with heavy hearts. Upon the hill, in the large stone house with the fluted columns and many gleaming, in-slanting windows, Abu Sa'id was struggling for life, and already the peasants felt his protective arm slipping from their shoulders.

In the two coffee houses on the main street of the village, the Israeli-Arabs gloomily discussed his state of health as they played their endless games of backgammon and puffed on their *nargilehs*. They were also worried by the thought that there might be war. They did not want to flee across the border, nor, if Israel were attacked, to take up arms against their brother Arabs. The Israeli government did not require it of them. They sighed heavily; it was truly a *shaitan's* trap they were caught in.

Farther down the street, the Arab women workers of the Dress Cooperative caught a glimpse of the *kibbutz* truck, with Ora at the wheel. Between her and young Dr. Erni sat her grandfather, old Noah, the *Mukhtar* of the neighboring Jewish *kibbutz*. It was Dr. Erni's second visit to Abu Sa'id that day, and it meant that Abu Sa'id's health had worsened.

In the large stone house, with the many gleaming windows, the eyes of those in the sickroom were riveted on Dr. Erni as he examined the patient.

Khalil, the son of Abu Sa'id, a thickset man with a beaked nose and shrewd eyes in a fleshy, pock-marked face, watched the young doctor, as he slid his stethoscope over the bared chest, and thought it unseemly of Ora to stand at the bedside while his father was thus exposed. But then she had always been a bold one and unconcerned about the proprieties.

He did not like her. She was brainy and too positive, and such Jewish women always made him uncomfortable. The elders of his *hamula* disliked her, too; she had great influence over the village women. She had stirred them up to demand classes (a school for mothers of children!), stirred them up to vote in every election, and always for something costly like those sewing machines. And before you could shout Enough! There was the Dress Cooperative right here in Umm Tubas! Socialism!

Why was Dr. Erni so long at his probing? It was chilly in the room, with the wind blowing in from the windows which Ora had thrown open immediately after she came. Old Noah, her grandfather, sat close to the bed, worriedly studying Dr. Erni's face.

Khalil should have sent for the Arab physician in Nazareth. His kinsmen had been appalled at his failure to do this, but his father had insisted on the *kibbutz* doctor and, in this house as well as in Umm Tubas, the Old Warrior's wish was law. For one thing, Khalil thought that Dr. Erni, for all his learning in America, was too young to be relied upon.

It had been awesome and rather frightening— the mechanisms that Dr. Erni had brought—the wires that he had attached to the sick body—the long hose of the oxygen tank that he clamped to the face. All this had restored the stilled heart so that it was beating again, but it had disquieted Khalil. He thought the machinery sacrilegious and obscene and that, in permitting this to be done to his father, he was challenging Allah's will.

And yet, when early this morning Dr. Erni had taken the machinery back to the *kibbutz,* Khalil had been frantic that, without them, his father would die. Be that as it may, he had no choice but to believe what the doctor was now saying, that there was a chance that his father would recover. *Inshallah!*

From the flatness of his unpillowed bed, Abu Sa'id saw first the white ruff of hair like a halo above the ears, then the anxious eyes, the ruddy face, the round nose and the hard, stubborn jaw. Noah. With whom he had shared a troubled childhood, war in their adolescent and middle years, and now an old age of much woe and some few joys. Noah, his twin soul.

Now Abu Sa'id shifted his eyes to Ora. A bold one, but splendidly alive. She was listening to Khalil with a faint smile, as if with a concealed doubt. Clever girl, Ora. Noah was gullible and accepted everyone at his own value, but not Ora. With her direct, questioning look she could take the measure of a man—and fault him.

The low murmur of voices made him feel drowsy. He stirred, and instantly Dr. Erni, who had been writing on a pad, darted to his side.

"I want pillows and a drink."

"Certainly a drink. I am prescribing a diet for you. It may not be to your taste, but you will gain strength from it." Ora bent over Abu Sa'id with a glass filled with pale amber water, from which a glass tube protruded. With one hand, she gently raised his head, and with the other, inserted the tube into his mouth. He had no choice but to suck in the warm, insipid tea. He growled with distaste.

At the familiar sound, Noah bounced to his feet, his face beaming, and he paced the room to contain his joy. It had been unbearable that his old friend was in the grip of death while he himself was in good health.

Abu Sa'id's eyes swiveled about to keep Noah in view and he grumbled, "You old goat! You make me dizzy with your prancing. I nearly died, and where were you?"

"Here! Suffering with you!" Noah took Abu Sa'id's hand and pressed it between his palms. "You won't die until I do. And God isn't ready for me yet, or he would have taken me when the mine exploded."

Ora wiped the drops of tea that slithered down the side of Abu Sa'id's mouth. She noticed that the eyes in the hawklike face were now clear and had regained their sharpness—a sure sign of recovery. She felt heartened; while these two old ones lived, all was right in her world.

Abu Sa'id fixed his eyes on Ora.

"Did you get the work-study group together yet?"

"We're voting on the project tonight," she replied and, taking the empty glass and the diet Erni had written, she left the room.

Presently Fared came in. Nodding to the three men, he walked directly to his grandfather. He bent down, took his hand and kissed it reverently. "You look much better, my grandfather."

"That is because I am not sick," the old man said. "Did you win the game over the ones from Haifa?"

"I didn't play. How could I, with my mind in this room?" A faint smile touched the sallow face. "Have you been studying your Hebrew? The examination is not far off."

"Yes, I have been working hard. I'm due at my tutor's house soon."

As Fared spoke, the old man's eyes kept closing and he mumbled something inaudible. Then, after a heavy sigh, he said, *"Ma'a salameh,"* and dozed off.

Fared shook hands with Noah and wondered if he should join his father and Dr. Erni, who stood talking at the window. He admired the young physician who had, several months ago, returned from a residency at a major hospital in New York. He was only of medium height, but he carried his shoulders erectly, and this made him seem taller. With his blond hair cut close to his elongated head, his fair complexion, blue eyes and narrow, but shapely nose, he looked far more German than Jewish.

Dr. Erni put in two afternoons at the Umm Tubas Clinic near the secondary school and did not consider it beneath him to join the boys in a game of basketball—and he was very good at it. Fared ventured over to the two men and, addressing himself to Dr. Erni, remarked, in his faltering Hebrew, that his grandfather looked much better, that he was alert and had even asked him if he had won the Nazareth-Haifa game.

"Your Hebrew has improved," Dr. Erni said.

"I've been boning up for the exams at Hebrew University."

"What science courses will you take?"

"That's what I wanted to speak to you about. I'll take those that will be required when I go on to medical college." He was aware that his father's eyebrows had risen almost to his hairline at this news. He had intended telling him earlier about his decision for a medical career, but hadn't because, when Fared asked his father if he ever visited Ibrahim Tabari (intending in some way to lead up to Laila), his father had frowned. "Tabari? Is he of our sinew?" It had angered Fared because his father knew very well that Ibrahim Tabari did not belong to any *hamula.*

Glancing at his watch, Erni said, "Fared, I have to rush off to the clinic, but see me here tomorrow morning around seven, and we'll talk about it."

Seven in the morning was still the middle of the night to Fared, but he said, "I'll be waiting for you."

Ora came back into the room and the three from the *kibbutz* left.

As they hurried down the sloping path to the truck, Ora asked, "Erni, it's still very serious, isn't it?"

"Yes, but, for a man in his middle seventies, Abu Sa'id has remarkable resilience."

Slowing down at a crossroad, she turned into the long main street of the Arab village and wheeled to the curb at the clinic, a square-shaped cement building with Arabic lettering on its large window. The high-pitched shouts of boys at play reached them from the secondary school sports yard farther up the street. Directly opposite the clinic was the auto and tractor repair shop owned by the three Tabari brothers, and Noah said he would drop in on them for a bit.

Dribbling a basketball down the street, a young Arab of about eighteen looked up as Ora parked the truck. He was short and wiry, with a massive head from which thick black hair sprang up wildly. He wore a striped T-shirt, which was shredded at the elbow, and his rumpled jeans were mud-spattered. The eyes in his thin, intelligent face were sharp, and held a hint of disdain for the three in the truck. Erni called out, "*Shalom,* Abdul. Been practicing?"

"That's obvious, isn't it?" Abdul answered curtly, and walked on, still dribbling the ball.

"I deserved that," Erni said, a little sheepishly. "Abdul is one of the few boys here that I just can't reach. Yet before I left for the United States he was friendly. He'd let me give him pointers on basketball. He's a brainy kid—said he wanted to get a higher education—and aimed for a career in science. The others come to me with their bruises and ailments and ask me questions about sex, but not Abdul."

He turned around, and at that moment Abdul turned also. Seeing Erni looking at him, he shrugged and moved on.

Pensively, Erni said, "I liked him—thought he was the best of the lot—and now he turns away when I come on the playing field. I can't dismiss him as a frustrated Arab—it's more complex than that. I was told he'd written a poem consisting of three words—Gamal Abdel Nasser—but that's only a fraction of a clue. . . ."

"Nasser is welcome to him," Ora said dryly.

"That is a snap judgment and solves nothing," Erni said sharply, as he hopped from the truck and helped Noah down.

Leaning out of the cab, she kissed him. "I deserved that," she said, and drove off. Farther up the street, she saw the shimmering orbs of light from the window of the Dress Cooperative, where the Arab women were still at work. It was too late now to visit; the women would detain her with their personal problems, the manager was sure to complain of one thing or another, and work was piling up for her in the *kibbutz*.

Outside the coffee house, the familiar group of Arabs sat at tables, and several of them nodded to her. The radio was blasting out the usual five o'clock threat from Cairo: ". . . the Arab people want to fight. . . . We have been waiting for the right time . . . when we will be completely ready. . . . Now the war will be total. . . . Its objective will be the annihilation of Israel."

She pressed down hard on the accelerator, and the roar, as she sped up the hill, drowned out the radio voice. She thought about Fared, pleased at his eagerness to join the work-study group, but she was of two minds about it. He was the grandson of Abu Sa'id, and this, should the project be accepted at tonight's meeting, would be an inducement for other Arab parents to send their young to the *kibbutz*. But Fared lacked the stability of Laila Tabari. If the field work and the study course proved too hard for him, he might drop out, and then the others would, too.

Now the road coiled upward in sudden twists and demanded her concentration. The bluish gray that preceded sundown silvered the leaves of the olive trees in an Arab field. Clumps of bushes on both sides of the road obscured the sharp turns, and she braked with a hard thwack on the horn at a hiker—Adam Posner, a long stick of a boy, topped by a shaggy mass of flaxen hair. She was in no mood for his sarcastic remarks or his stormy silences.

She honked again, gently now, and drew alongside him. He ignored her. "Adam, it's easier to ride over these hills." She spoke in English—a concession.

"I prefer to walk," he said glumly.

"So do I, but it's getting late and these hill roads, as you know, can be very confusing."

He climbed in and sat close to the door, to put as much space as possible between them. Ora was part of the establishment here which he hated as much as the one in Poland. And Adam relished his hates.

Ora ventured again. "If the vote for the Arab Work-Study Project goes favorably tonight, you will have several Arab boys for roommates."

"What about Yoram and Itzhak? Have they complained about me?"

"Should they have?"

He shrugged.

"They will soon go into the army. You will find Fared a likable young man. He has just completed secondary school and is a candidate at Hebrew University."

"An Arab?" Adam's tone was one of disbelief rather than curiosity.

"Why not—if he can pass the entrance exams?"

"I thought, well. . . ." And he shrugged off the rest.

"If they, like the Jews, meet the requirements and can pay the tuition, they are accepted. Some of them get scholarships."

She smiled at a small victory; Adam was asking questions. True, they were of a negative nature, but that was because, in Poland, he had been indoctrinated against Israel. Trying to bring the talk to a personal level, she offered, "Aviva thinks your Hebrew has improved."

Not quite true; Aviva had said, "Adam is tops in

math and chemistry. He has a brain and could learn Hebrew easily, if he didn't resist it so. He still thinks he is returning to Poland."

Adam was so bitter about what had happened to him in Poland, so brainwashed by the anti-Semitic campaign, that he loathed being a Jew. He resented his father for bringing him to Israel and detested his mother because she had willingly consented to Adam being taken to Israel.

"But why should Arabs come to stay in the *kibbutz?*" Adam broke the silence. "They hate Israe-lis."

Hate, Ora knew, was the operative word in his vocabulary.

"Some do," Ora admitted. "They resent us for winning two wars. But there are many Arabs who believe we can live together in peace. There are Arab youths studying in the *kibbutz* secondary schools. It is important that we learn to know each other. Wouldn't you like to be a friend to an Arab?"

Adam shrugged. "It makes no difference to me."

Whatever was done for Adam made no difference to him. He was living in a vacuum filling up with self-pity and frustration. She tried again. "You will like Fared. He is the grandson of our friend, Abu Sa'id. Fared speaks English and is very good at sports. And there is Adnan Tabari, who writes poetry. His sister, Laila, will come, too. She graduated with honors from the secondary school in Nazareth."

"They sound too good to be Arabs."

Ora gave up in disgust. They were now at the turn of the road into Tel Hashava.

She sighed at the thought of the meeting that

night, and she felt too tired to cope with the arguments that were certain to erupt over the Arab project. Had Aviva tackled those who were against it? Amitai, particularly?

3

Student Power Confronts
the *Kibbutz* Cowboy

Amitai, the *kibbutz* cowboy, was relaxing on the lawn in front of the dining hall, his back against a flowering jacaranda tree. He saw Aviva detaching herself from a group of youths, and knew at once that he was in for her special attention. Moshe, her shadow, followed but, at a few words from her, he drew back and began tootling on his harmonica.

Pulling his cowboy hat over his face, Amitai folded his arms and gave what he thought would be a convincing picture of a man napping. For the first time in her life, Aviva would hear a very positive no from him. On the upper field, where he grazed the cattle, he had taught her to ride a horse, taught her to swing a lasso into descending circles, and spent countless evenings spinning tales or reading to her through all her childhood ailments. He was willing to die for her, but he would not vote for the Arab Work-Study Project.

He felt the brim of his hat turned up and he looked into a face that glowed with youth. In the last rays of the sun, her red hair blazed like whorls of flame and her sea-green eyes danced saucily at him. She was such an imp of a girl that it was difficult to believe she had a will of iron. Ora's daughter.

Positively he would say no! He scowled.

"Brrr! You frighten me—you look so fierce!" she said and shivered.

"Vivi, spare me your arguments," he growled, as she took off his hat and put it on her head, and crouched down beside him on the lawn. "I heard them before. I will vote no to the Arab boys. Positively."

"Amitai, why should I argue with you? I only wanted to ask if you heard the broadcast about the offer made by the Israeli-Arab boys to rebuild Kibbutz Dan?"

"Who needs their good deeds? They could be fatal."

"Tell me, Amitai, how can a good deed be fatal?"

"By believing them, when they say they want to help, when they really mean to spy, to steal, to kill."

"But how can we ever be friends if we don't give them a chance to prove they mean what they say?"

"That's exactly what those across the borders want—to prove that they mean what they say by killing us," he said and rubbed meaningfully at his fractured jaw.

"But I'm not talking about Syrian Arabs! I'm

talking about *Israeli*-Arabs who want to help rebuild what the Syrians destroyed in Kibbutz Dan."

"Then let these Arabs go tell the Syrians to stop shelling us," he said and snatched back his hat and slammed it over his face.

Aviva despaired. It was no use. Amitai would spark the opposition at the meeting and turn the vote against the project. She should have insisted that Yoram speak with Amitai—he was the brainy one. But the others had said that she, being Amitai's pet, would be more persuasive.

If only he would stay away from the meeting! She tried again. "Amitai, they are going to show an American western tonight."

"I saw it twice already," he muttered from under his hat.

"It's no use, Yoram," Aviva said, as they came into the meeting hall. "Amitai won't listen to reason. He rubs at his jaw—and that means the subject, like his mind, is closed."

"Don't worry. I think we have enough votes," he assured her.

The hall was festive with *Purim* decorations. Colored paper lanterns, balloons and gay streamers fluttered from a wire strung across the ceiling. Paper chains of every color festooned the walls, under which hung caricatures of Haman, the Hitler of ancient Persia, and other historic tyrants. These were drawn by the *kibbutz* members and the teenage pupils. One section was given over to the young set and Aviva was impressed with their use of imaginative designs and vivid colors.

"Emmi lets the little ones go wild with paint and brush," Yoram commented. He was referring to his mother, who worked with the children.

"She's absolutely right," Aviva said. "At their age, you don't tamper with their creative impulses."

"That's why they're such little monsters. They need discipline, and my mother can't impose it," he said.

"She certainly can—and does!" Aviva retorted. "She does it so quietly the kids don't know its discipline, but they obey. Who do you think civilized you?"

"That is debatable," he grinned. "Did Ora get back from Umm Tubas? How is Abu Sa'id?"

"Much better. She seemed sort of distracted. She brought Adam home from one of his wanderings."

"Now that would distract anybody," Yoram said.

On the platform where Aviva and Yoram sat between Avram, the secretary, and Pinhas, the treasurer, Aviva tried to keep her eyes from straying to Erni in the first row. She still smarted from his remark before the meeting began when, just as she and Yoram were taking the seats that Emmi had saved for them, Avram called them to sit on the platform. Erni had said to her, "Ah, so they've elevated you to the rank of elder statesman!" She replied icily, "Not quite. That is only a token gesture to student power."

He never teased the other seventeen-year-olds, and he listened seriously to them, but he made her feel like an idiot child.

Noah, her great-grandfather, whose tall white

ruff of hair fanned upward, blocked off Amitai, who was sitting directly behind him. She felt relieved because, until it was her turn to speak, she would not be disconcerted by his sarcastic staring. Next to Erni sat his sister Emmi. She looked like him, but her features were more delicate and she wore her light brown hair in a braided coronet.

Ora was making a report on the needs of the grade school. The *kibbutz* members listened quietly —Ora never wasted words—but Aviva felt they were becoming restless; the meeting had dragged on too long.

It was late when Avram announced the last item on the agenda—the Arab Work-Study Project—and, to Aviva's surprise, no one rose to leave. There was a shifting about on seats, some grumbling, and Amitai let out a yawn like the braying of a mule. There was laughter, but everyone remained in the room.

Ora rose to speak. The project had been initiated by Kibbutz Artzi, and its success encouraged her to propose that it be accepted here. This meant boarding a group of young Israeli-Arabs, for one year, who were to attend classes with their *kibbutz* peers, participate in all the social and sports activities and, together with their classmates, work four hours a day—for which they would be paid a few pounds.

Considering the recent planting of a mine in the *kibbutz*, and the Syrian shelling of Kibbutz Dan, Ora admitted that accepting the project tested their belief in Jewish-Arab amity. She reminded them that a few nights ago the six o'clock "Voice of Israel" radio broadcaster announced that a group of Israel-

Arab youths had volunteered to help in the rebuild-
ing of Kibbutz Dan, and Aviva would now read the
letter they had sent.

Faces brightened as Aviva rose. She stood out-
wardly poised with assurance, but inwardly she
trembled. She saw that Erni was about to light his
pipe but, smiling at Aviva, he put it back in his
pocket. It eased her, but her voice quavered at the
first few words.

Dear Friends!

We would very much like to visit your kibbutz *and express
our solidarity and to give you all the help we can.*

*We have not forgotten the goodwill and solidarity you
showed toward us when some of our homes in [Israeli] Arab
el-Suwa'ed were demolished under various pretexts, and
your struggle as a* kibbutz *and as individuals to stop the dem-
olition.*

*No one knows better than us how terrible it is when your
home is destroyed in front of your eyes or when it is threatened
with destruction. But we know it is even more terrible when
there is a danger of the people living in the homes being killed.
We were shocked to the core by the indiscriminate shelling of*
kibbutz *children, mothers and farmers. It is awesome that this
awful deed did not lead to loss of life. This does not mean that
we forget the bereaved families in both Syria and Israel, who
have sustained such a great human loss.*

Aviva paused briefly and let her eyes sweep over
the audience with a smile that hinted that the best
was yet to come. She resumed reading at a slower
pace to give the climax a greater impact.

*We feel deeply that all citizens of Israel share a common
destiny, no matter to which people they belong.*

*Accept our sincerest sympathy for the experience you have
undergone. Let us work together so that this act will not be
repeated, so that our country will attain peace with the Arab
countries, which are not alien to us, so that the Israeli farmers*

and the Syrian fellaheen *will be able to till their fields in peace
and quiet.*

> Greetings from a group of young
> people from the villages:
> (Israeli-Arab el-Suwa'ed,
> Jet, Ramm-el-Fahm, and Barta'a).

There was silence when Aviva finished reading. Then the clapping broke out. Aviva's face was radiant as she returned to her seat—the letter had won them over!

Now Yoram rose. He waited for the applause to cease, then spoke, "You already know that we of the secondary school have voted unanimously for this project, so I will speak briefly."

"We heard it already! We heard!" Amitai roared out.

Noah swiveled around and silenced him with a loud, *"Sheket!"*

Unabashed, Yoram went on, "We have had students from Ghana, Nigeria, Ceylon, Indonesia and many other African and Asian countries, living here to study our *kibbutz* way of life; so why not have our Arab neighbors? We don't ask that you love your neighbors as yourselves. We only ask that you give us the opportunity to know each other so that we can be friends instead of strangers. As it said in the letter, 'all citizens of Israel share a common destiny, no matter to which people they belong,' so at least let's get to know each other. Who knows, we may even get to like each other."

There was laughter, and it drowned out Amitai's resounding snort.

"Vote! Vote!" A few members cried out, while

an enraged Amitai jumped to his feet, shouting, "I haven't spoken yet!"

Malka, Amitai's plump, good-natured wife, tugged at his arm and when he subsided, she offered an amendment that limited the number of Arabs accepted into the *kibbutz* to seven. Ora was appalled—so small a number would be ineffectual. In her mind, she had already selected twelve from Umm Tubas alone, and a similar number from other Arab villages.

The amendment was accepted.

Amitai was still in a rage as he stomped out. Aviva seized his arm. "Don't be angry. You will see—it will work out just fine!"

"From your mouth to God's ears, but nowadays He is deaf to us," and he jerked his arm away.

Watching her as he lighted his pipe, Erni said in English, "You can't win them all, Vivi. But you did splendidly."

Flustered at his unexpected compliment, she said tartly, "Thank you! All I needed was that letter and your approval to get results!" She turned away, feeling wretched at her childish remark and thinking, small wonder that he considers me immature!

4

A New Way of Life

"Oh, I'm so excited I can hardly breathe! Aren't you, Ayesha?" Laila asked, as she and her friend climbed into the cab of the *kibbutz* truck.

Ora, who had just picked up the seven Arab youths at the Umm Tubas Clinic, smiled knowingly and predicted the girl's reply.

"I'm too nervous to be excited," Ayesha said as she fussed with the folds of her print dress.

The reply, Ora thought, revealed the essential difference between the two girls whom she had known since their infancy. Laila Tabari was alert and responsive to any new experience, while Ayesha Ailani shrank from the unfamiliar. Laila had a deep and questing mind that set her apart from the other girls in her village.

They were the only girls of the seventeen-to-eighteen-year group in Umm Tubas who had been selected for the project and, while Laila's father had eagerly consented, Ayesha's father had, at first, refused, as it was not the custom for Arab girls to sleep in other villages unless it was in the homes of their kin.

Ibrahim Tabari, who had been active with Noah and Ora in the old Jewish-Arab unity movement when the country was under British rule, persuaded Ailani to permit his daughter to join the group. He yielded on condition that Ora give her word to keep the boys separated from the girls. Ora gave her word, and now Fared and four youths sat in the rear of the truck on the nailed down, backless bench.

Fared listened abstractedly to the three in the cab. The truck kept jolting over potholes in the road, and he wished that Ora had not objected to his bringing his sports car. She had even objected to his camera!

Lately he detected a change in Ora's attitude toward him. He couldn't pinpoint it to anything specific. She seemed indifferent to his joining the group. The work, she said, was strenuous, and life in the *kibbutz* was quite spartan; he would miss the luxuries to which he was accustomed.

But Laila was going, and this had resolved him.

Would his father raise the issue of his marriage to Laila when the *hamula* met this month? He had asked his father to visit Tabari but was told it would be against tradition to discuss anything with Tabari until the *hamula* had met and made a decision.

What right had they to reach into his private life

to determine its course? He thought it was time for this archaic tribal system to be abandoned.

In all the village, there was no one like Laila. She was "the one with the wise old head," who could explain the most complex problem, could cut through to the core of an involved theory, could smooth away a hurt. He felt himself standing taller because, while his friends admired Laila, she loved only him.

He was at ease with her as with no one else. She knew, merely by looking at him, when he was boasting or telling one of his small lies. With her he did not need to play a role, as he did with Abdul. With her, he was at ease with himself and happy.

An arm slid around his shoulder. It was Adnan, Laila's brother, and he felt a little annoyed. Ibrahim Tabari had sent his seventeen-year-old son along to keep a watchful eye on Fared and Laila, he felt certain. Adnan was friendly, but they had nothing in common; he disliked sports and had what Fared considered feminine interests—reading, music, and he wrote poetry! With his soft eyes and small, fine features, he even looked like a girl.

"I wish I were a week older," Adnan said moodily.

"Why?"

"Because—because they are strangers to me now."

"Nonsense!" Fared waved away his fears. "You know Dr. Erni, old Noah, Ora. Jews are like us—only they're Western."

Adnan frowned. Fared never bothered to reach deep into his mind, for an answer, as Laila did.

He dropped his arm from Fared's shoulders and resumed his brooding thoughts, wondering if those at the *kibbutz* would scorn him because of his artificial leg, although he could even dance now that Dr. Erni had taught him muscle control. He had dedicated his last poem to him.

Also, he owed Fared a poem for risking his life to save him when the mine at the demilitarized zone exploded. If Fared hadn't come along at that precise moment in his father's car, and reached for him across the danger belt, and rushed him to the hospital, all his blood would have oozed out and he surely would have died.

"But what had you been doing in that area when you knew it was a danger zone?" Laila had asked when, after the operation, he had been sent to the Hadassah Hospital's special therapy department for amputees.

"I—I—was working on a poem. I was walking and wasn't aware where I was," Adnan replied, and felt guilty over the lie ever since. He never told her about Abdul being with him, because she'd ask more questions about what Abdul was doing there.

Now Laila was asking Ora if, when they went home for their holy day on Friday, they were expected back in the *kibbutz* on the Jewish Sabbath, or on Sunday. Fared shifted his position to listen to them.

He asked, "Ora, wouldn't it make it easier for everyone if your people celebrated Sabbath when we do ours—on Friday?"

Ora was about to answer when Laila said, with

an edge of annoyance, "Fared, if I didn't know your kind of humor, I'd say that you were a bigot!"

"Why a bigot?" Fared asked, chagrined. The four youths, sitting beside him on the bench, grinned as if expecting him to be outwitted by Laila's more logical mind.

"Because we Moslems are a minority—only one-seventh of the world's population," she replied. "Why should we ask non-Moslems to change their holy day to ours?"

While Fared's question was perhaps only an innocent impertinence, Ora thought it revealed a trend in his thinking. The Radio Cairo kept hammering away daily with advice to Israeli-Arabs: "Sow confusion and fear among the enemy, no matter how small. It all adds up and weakens their morale." Fared, she observed through the windshield mirror, looked crestfallen after Laila's rebuke.

"Adnan, I brought your poem." Laila raised her voice over the grinding of the engine, as it began the steep climb to the *kibbutz*. "Ora liked it very much and said she will translate it the first chance she gets, so it can be read at the *kibbutz*."

"It isn't good—you shouldn't have brought it," he said, and felt immensely pleased that she had. On his lap lay the *mizmar* that Ora had urged him to bring, and he picked it up and blew softly into it, thinking, perhaps it will be all right for him in the *kibbutz*.

As the truck ground up the hill, toward a cluster of sand-colored cottages with sloping, orange-tiled roofs, Aviva came running and leaped on the running board. "*Ima!* What took you so long?"

"I told you never to do this when the truck is moving!" Ora scolded. "Two boys misunderstood where the collection point was." She introduced Laila and Ayesha.

"Welcome! You are most welcome!" Aviva said, in English.

"We are glad to be here," Laila replied, in Hebrew, warmed by the girl's friendliness.

Ora had asked the students who would share rooms with the Arabs to assemble at the office building, and now they stood outside waiting with Noah and Erni. When the truck drew up to a stop before them, Erni reached for the girls' bundles and helped them down.

"Welcome! Welcome twice!" Noah said, in Arabic. He was a familiar figure in Umm Tubas, and the youths felt at ease with him. He began the introductions.

With his eager grin and spectacles awry, Moshe jostled through to the center of the group and stammered, when Ora looked questioningly at him, "I . . . I am the official greeter for my class." He went around shaking hands with the youths but only smiled at the two girls with whom Aviva had linked arms.

Ora was pleased at the friendliness all around, although Adam Posner looked on with a detached air. Ayesha lost her nervousness when a girl emerged, introduced herself as her roommate and, after a vigorous handshake, relieved her of the bundle she was holding.

Ora announced that there would be no work for the group that day, so they could acquaint themselves with the *kibbutz*, at which Fared let out a cheer.

Aviva turned to Laila and, taking her bundle, said, "Let's go to our room!" They set off along the flagstone walk.

They came to a long, two-storied building, whose center arched over a shop and a coffee lounge. Ramps at both ends of the building led to a second floor that was glass-enclosed. "That's our dining hall up there," Aviva offered.

"It's very modern and beautiful," Laila said. "I'm not often impressed with modern buildings. They're unusual, but too cold and without grace."

"You must have been in Tel Aviv," Aviva said, and they both burst into laughter.

Laila noted the lawns between the cottages that were edged with flower beds and the colorful drapes at open windows. She caught a glimpse of paintings and bookshelves on the walls, and thought how pleasant it was in this village.

They went past a squared-off barricade, below which men were digging a wide trench. "We are building another shelter," Aviva said, adding in a matter-of-fact tone, "should there be war."

"Oh, I hope not!" Laila exclaimed. "There should not be war between brother-peoples. It is—insane!"

Aviva looked thoughtfully at her, then pressed her cheek hard against Laila's. "Oh, but I like you! Ora said I would!"

They came to several flat-roofed concrete and glass buildings that faced each other across a wide paved walk. "Our secondary school," Aviva offered. "The grade school is at the far side of the dwellings.

But here we are!" And she led her up a path to a cottage, and into a large, square-shaped room.

It contained three studio-beds ranged along a wall, with a chest of drawers next to each one. The rust-and-brown-colored bedspreads of geometric designs matched the drapes at the windows. In the center of the room stood chairs around a table which held a fluted glass bowl of fruit.

A blouse and shorts lay crumpled on one bed tangled up with a towel, a pair of sneakers and a few books. "That's Dvora's," Aviva said. "She's usually tidy, but she must have been late for kitchen duty when she came from class."

"It is all lovely," Laila said. "But please speak Hebrew. I need the practice."

"Okay. I think Adnan is very sweet," Aviva said.

"Yes, he is a fine boy."

"Did Ora tell you the program?"

"Yes, we have a choice of subjects: math, chemistry, biology, literature, history, economics, language. Ora knows I can stay only one term—I am to take entrance exams at Hebrew University," Laila said.

"Guess what school I'll apply to after I graduate," Aviva said, and she whirled about on the toes of one foot and ended in an arabesque. Laila applauded when, laughing, she dropped into a chair.

"Ballet, of course!" Laila said.

"First, I must go into the army and then, perhaps, I'll go to America for my ballet training. My father is an American. He said he can get me into a good school, though he thinks another ballet dancer is the last thing Israel needs."

"I don't agree with him!" Laila exclaimed.

"Convince me why you do not agree with him."

"If you need convincing it means you are not certain."

"Oh, but I am!" Aviva said in great earnest. "Only, I want to hear another Israeli tell me that it's all right to want such a career—in these times."

"Well . . ." Laila's brow furrowed, and her fingers pressed against it as if prodding an answer. "Well, art is a symbol of civilization, and I think dancing is a most beautiful art form. And we need all the art forms to neutralize what is wrong in the world. Don't you agree?"

"I agree! Absolutely I agree! Oh, we'll get along splendidly!"

One by one the Arab youths were escorted to the dormitories and, at the office building, only Fared and Adnan remained to be taken to theirs. Adnan's roommates, after hearty greetings with pincerlike handshakes that had nearly crushed his fingers, and with a rush of words too fast for him to understand, had hurried away. Dr. Erni, whose welcoming smile had eased their nervousness, said, "Your roommates are working on an experiment in the lab and had to rush back, but I'll take you to your room and stay a bit. You can entertain me with your *mizmar*."

"I'm not really good enough at it. . . ."

"When I want to hear a professional, I go to a concert. Between concerts, I'll be content to listen to your playing."

Adnan gave a delighted titter. Yes, he would like it in the *kibbutz*.

His two roommates were an odd pair, Fared thought. Adam Posner, the tall blond one, was neither man nor boy, and aloof, while Yoram was friendly, but had an appraising look that conveyed a hint of suspicion. He was built like a young bull— stocky and muscular—and Fared wondered if he was good at sports.

"I've some lab work to finish," Yoram said. "Adam will take you to our room. My bed's at the window, but if you like, you can have it. See you later." With a smile that was surprisingly sweet for one so rough-mannered, he strode away.

"He is always busy, that one," Adam offered, as he led Fared toward their cottage. They passed a lane bordered on both sides with eucalyptus trees, beyond which stood a long, barracklike building. A truck drove up and parked before it. About a dozen men and women carrying farm tools alighted, went inside the building and emerged empty handed.

Although it was a cool morning, their faces were streaked with sweat and their khaki shirts clung wetly to their backs. They looked tired, as if they'd been working for many hours, Fared observed, and it was only nine o'clock! How early do they begin their work here? He wondered how early he'd have to rise and what kind of work he'd have to do. He was about to ask Adam, when a horde of youngsters erupted from the school building and scrambled past him to a bus, nearly tumbling him onto the first step of the underground shelter.

"They do not discipline them here. They have no manners," Adam said.

Accustomed to his own room with its handsome

furnishings, Fared thought the one he was to share particularly uninviting; there were three untidily made studio-beds, three crude chests, a table with chairs, and an uncarpeted stone floor. He put his valise on the bed which Adam motioned was to be his, and began to unpack. He felt uncomfortable with his roommate, who kept pacing about.

"Where do you come from?" Fared asked.

"Poland."

"Didn't you like it there?"

Adam's face tightened. Then, when Fared removed an aluminum-sheathed radio from his valise, Adam picked it up, looked admiringly at it and flicked on a knob.

"What was said?" Adam asked, when Fared switched it off.

"The usual. There will be war. Do you like sports?"

"In Poland I was quite good at soccer."

"Soccer is my game, too. That, and racing my sports car."

"My hobby is photography," Adam said and nodded at the camera on his chest of drawers.

Fared took it in his hands and examined it, and Adam said irritably, "Don't click—it's loaded."

"I didn't intend to," Fared said coldly. It was only a few minutes past nine, and already he felt ill at ease and discouraged. In the awkward silence that followed, he thought that if Yoram was as unfriendly as this one, he might leave even before Friday. Just then a flute throbbed a few notes into the air. Adnan with his *mizmar*.

"It sounds like the Jews wailing at prayer," Adam said. "Sometimes Yoram tunes in on Amman or Cairo, and it sounds like that. Is all Arab music sad?"

"Of course not! Some of our songs are very gay—our dance music especially," Fared replied edgily. Opening the door, he crossed the small corridor and went into Adnan's room. Adnan smiled a greeting with his eyes, as he fingered his flute, and Dr. Erni welcomed him into the room with a wave of his pipe.

Fared took an orange from the plate of fruit which the doctor had pushed toward him, and sat down beside him on the bed. He felt relieved to find himself among friends.

That night, in bed, Laila felt fatigued but pleasantly so, and much too stimulated to sleep. Had she come here only this morning? As was her habit with every new experience, she tried to arrange her impressions into some order, but they came at random, like a kaleidoscope that with a shake brings a new scene into view: the school buildings, the auditorium for concerts, plays, cinemas, meetings, the library and the dining halls. The *kibbutz* seemed to her like a human beehive, with people always in motion.

Soon after they arrived, Ora had brought her and Ayesha to the school. Except for the math and chemistry classes and the lab—where order and quiet prevailed—everywhere else seemed chaotic; the students held noisy discussions with each other or engaged in dialogues with the teachers. It was not at all like the convent classes she had been accustomed to.

When the periods ended, the students surrounded them with a friendliness that made her and Ayesha feel at ease. They asked questions about her school, and the subjects she had taken, and which European authors she had read, and if she liked Sartre. If Ora hadn't warned the students that they would be late for their next class, their questions, Laila felt certain, would reveal her ignorance; she had never read Sartre and very few of the authors they had mentioned.

When they came out of the building Ora told them that, despite the seeming disorder in the classrooms, there was a discipline at work—teaching them to think and to question was the basis of the learning process. Laila wondered how, in all this bedlam, they could concentrate or learn anything.

Also there was a problem, and it troubled her. All the pupils wore shorts: Were she and Ayesha expected to do the same? It was not the custom for Arab girls to thus expose themselves. Would Fared object?

In the evening there were more classes, adult and disciplined, briefly visited, and cultural clubs. And then she saw something that puzzled her and struck her rather unpleasantly: Some people had numbers stamped on their forearms.

She first saw it on the middle-aged woman who taught painting, and again on a woman who served them lunch, and then on the arm of the conductor who was rehearsing a choral group, and she wondered why the *kibbutz* had done this to some people and not to others.

When they went to their cottage to rest before dinner, she asked Aviva about this. "You mean you don't know?" Aviva's voice went high, and her eyes widened with astonishment. Laila shook her head.

"They were in Nazi concentration camps, where they were numbered, and it's indelible. The ones who came here after Hitler's defeat were the lucky ones, but six million Jews weren't so lucky. They were killed in the gas chambers and burnt to ashes."

Laila went numb with the horror of it.

"How is it you didn't know?" Aviva asked. "Hundreds of books were written about the Nazis."

"There were no such books in my school," Laila said, while Ayesha remarked, "It happened before we were born."

"That's no excuse," Laila said. "The history they taught us happened before we were born."

What came next in her mental kaleidoscope was the dining hall. At first the vast crowd, the clatter of dishes and clamor of voices overwhelmed her, and she saw that Ayesha, too, felt ill at ease. Aviva brought them to a table at which Ora, Erni, Noah and Avram sat. Laila knew them and quickly identified the woman with the braided hair around her head as Erni's sister. She felt drawn to this woman with the warm, quiet smile who kept pressing various dishes on her and Ayesha.

So many people came over to the table to be introduced that later, when someone asked her whether she enjoyed the food, she nodded, but could not recollect what she had eaten.

It surprised her how many different types of people there were, as if each was of a different nationality. There were some who looked as Arabic as those of her village and were, Aviva told her, Arab Jews from Yemen, Egypt, Morocco, Syria, Iraq and other Arab lands.

They were leaving the dining hall when Noah came with a man in tow who seemed to be protesting something. He wore a cowboy hat and his scarred face was tightly clenched. He looked, Laila thought, as if he grew up with anger.

Taking her arm, Noah said to the man, "This is Tabari's daughter. *Nu,* Amitai, did you ever think that Ibrahim, with his puss, would have such a beautiful girl?" And the man called Amitai narrowed his eyes and considered. Laila flushed.

"Amitai," Aviva said, and warned him with a look.

He gave a snort. "Noah, if you, with your ugly puss, could have such beauties as Ora and Aviva, miracles can happen to others, too."

Then, offering his hand, and it surprised Laila how gentle the leathery hand was when it enfolded hers, he asked, "Can you ride a horse?"

When she shook her head, Amitai said, "Tell Aviva to bring you to the plateau and I . . ." He stopped to glower at Aviva, who had put her hand to her mouth to stifle her giggling, "for Ibrahim Tabari's daughter I can always make an exception!" And he stomped away.

Oh, it would be very pleasant in the *kibbutz,* Laila thought.

And then it occurred to her that she hadn't seen Fared all day. Ora was keeping the promise she had given her parents to keep the sexes apart.

But Fared, she felt certain, would find a way to see her.

5

Off to a Good Start

The sun had already risen when Laila and Aviva set out to join the orchard workers. Yesterday, the senior and junior pupils of the secondary school had volunteered to plant fruit saplings in the upper field. Formerly this had been grazing land, and the work-study group worked with them clearing away stones and weeds.

Silently, the two girls walked to the machine shed. The air was crisp and fragrant with the scent of damp earth and flowers—their dew-drenched petals were already unfolding to the sun.

Reaching the nursery, Aviva snatched up a little toddler with a red bow in her dark curls and hugged her. The mother smiled tiredly, as she stifled a yawn, saying *"Boker tov!"* With a wide swing up in the air and down, Aviva deposited the child on the nursery veranda.

"You are like one big family," Laila observed. She was thinking of the evening meals, when the dining hall was lively with people exchanging tidbits of gossip or conversing with some seated several tables away. The clamor they raised no longer overwhelmed her.

"Well, we are, sort of. Of course it has its drawbacks, too," Aviva admitted. "You can't feel romantic about boys you grew up with since nursery days and who sat on the potty next to yours."

Laila blushed. Would she ever accustom herself to the frank and rather bold discussions that went on between girls, even when boys were present? She was still not accustomed to a free mingling of the sexes unchaperoned by adults.

The other night she was returning with Aviva and Ayesha to their rooms, after the folk dance, and Yoram and several others kept up a barrage of questions about Arab customs. Yoram had asked, "According to Moslem law, a man can have four wives. Would you be content to be one of the wives?"

Laila replied, "In most villages, the *fellaheen* is too poor to have more than one wife. And our young men are modern-minded. I would not marry one who isn't."

But she had qualms about all this. Fared was not pleased; he did not say this in words, but implied that both of them were surrendering to the customs in the *kibbutz.* Last night, in the gymnasium, she had worn Aviva's shorts, and Fared's disapproval was obvious by his cold stare.

The other afternoon, she had been pruning in the pear orchard and a sharp twig had cut her palm. Yoram came with a first-aid box and treated the bruise with medication, then covered it with a bandage. For all his gruff manners, his big paw of a hand had been light and gentle, and she had laughed off his silly concern. Fared had seen all this, and later Aviva remarked that it was not like Yoram to be silly, so perhaps he was in love with her. This embarrassed and worried Laila; what if Aviva's words got around to Fared!

Sometimes she felt as if she were living two unrelated lives—the one in Umm Tubas and quite another life in the *kibbutz*. It was like oscillating between two cultures. She sometimes wished her village would move a little faster into the twentieth century, and yet she felt at ease in its simple, unhurried life pattern. She appreciated *kibbutz* achievements, but she felt the tensions, and she did not know if this was because of their constant fear of war or because of the close, activated group living.

But she was thoroughly enjoying every minute of *kibbutz* life. Everyone seemed to *want* her, and the night before, in the gymnasium after the calisthenics, they had pulled her into a folk dance as if she belonged here. Life in the *kibbutz* was like an adventure—constantly unfolding new experiences.

The two girls were now within sight of the machine shed, and Laila came out of her musing to hear Aviva saying, "Race you to the trucks!" Laughing, they sprinted forward. A quick glance at the three Arab boys with Yoram told Laila that Fared and Adnan were late again.

Passing the half-finished concrete building, which was being constructed by four Arabs from Umm Tubas, Fared and Adnan called out a greeting. The workers wore white *kheffiyahs* wrapped around their heads, their strong teeth were like slashes of white in their smiling, nut-brown faces.

"So they're harnessing you to a plow!" one of them called out to Fared, while the other worker said, "You may not be as good as a mule but you're prettier!"

Laughing, Fared held up his hands, palms toward them. The blisters from clearing stones and weeds had become calluses.

Nearby, on the truck that had brought the Arab workers, a transistor radio blared out a lamenting song. It was, Adnan knew, being broadcast from the Arab department of the Israeli radio station, and it brought to his mind a matter that had been troubling him these past four days in the *kibbutz.*

"Fared, you ought not to tune in on Cairo."

"Why not?" Fared demanded irritably.

Troubled by this sudden change of mood, Adnan said, "Because—because you don't spit in the well from which you drink."

"But they themselves tune in on Cairo! Yoram does, and in the dining hall they listen and even make jokes."

"Well, they need to listen to know what's going on, but we shouldn't. Not here, anyway. It is—well—

as if we look to Cairo for leadership, don't you see?"
Adnan was beginning to feel nervous at Fared's
sudden anger.

"No, I don't see!" Fared snapped back, quicken-
ing his pace toward the trucks near the machine
sheds. The volunteers were waiting to be picked up,
and several of them were loading crates of saplings
and farming tools onto the trucks.

Laila detached herself from the group of girls
and greeted the two boys, asking, "What delayed
you?"

Adnan shrugged. His thigh pained and he'd had
trouble adjusting his artificial leg. If Fared hadn't
come, to see why he wasn't ready, and helped him,
he'd still be in his room. But if he told her that, she
would worry about his working in the field, and
certainly she would tell Ora.

"I didn't see either of you in the dining hall for
breakfast," she continued. "Have you eaten?"

"Yes," Fared said shortly, although his stomach
was grumbling with emptiness. He did not like it that
she had worn shorts last night, and had failed to note
his displeasure. Now she wore jeans. Allowable.

They climbed onto the trucks and Yoram, who
drove the one filled with saplings, called to Adnan to
sit with him in the cab.

Adnan felt immensely pleased about this. The
other day, after his two roommates had left to go into
the army, he wondered if he would have the cottage
to himself and was not relishing the prospect, when
Yoram moved in. He said, as he flung his belongings
on a cot, "Adam doesn't speak during the day, but he
makes up for it in his sleep. Loud, and in Polish yet!"

Smiling, Adnan swung himself into the cab as if the sudden stabs of pain in his thigh weren't happening. The trucks began climbing toward the upper reaches of the *kibbutz*. A panoramic view of the valley spread out before him, with the houses of Umm Tubas, snuggled like sugar cubes into the hills at the far south, and the vegetable fields of the *kibbutz* closer by. The cylindrical-shaped silo thrust white and tall against the cloudless sky. In the sun, the jets of water that sprouted from the holes in the raised pipes looked like flowing crystal. The movable pipes were raised on Y-shaped poles, about three feet off the ground, and ran between rows of cabbages, cucumbers, eggplants, pumpkins and radishes.

Adnan wondered if the work-study group would be invited to stay over the Jewish Sabbath when they would celebrate the last day of their *Purim* festival. He had seen the pupils rehearsing a play for the event—a satire on the hippies of San Francisco—and he had listened to a choral group practicing, and it all sounded very jolly. Also, there would be a campfire to end the holiday, and he had never been to one.

Perhaps, if he hinted to Yoram or Ora . . .

With his spade, Fared kept jabbing at the earth to make saucer-shaped holes for the saplings. It was hard work and very monotonous. Although the sun at his back was only mildly warm, sweat dripped down his face and into his eyes, stinging them. He was in an irritable mood. Twice that morning Ora had told him that the hole he was digging was not in line with the others. Her voice was low, so that the others did not hear, but he resented criticism, and felt mortified.

His watch told him that he had a full hour's work before the noon meal, but his stomach was growling with hunger. In the next row, Yoram had stopped to talk to Laila. Now he put his hand on her back, just under the shoulders, and the other hand over hers on the handle of the spade. He was probably telling her, as he had told Fared earlier, to let the back and shoulders, rather than the arms, do the work; it was less tiring. Fared thought Yoram was prolonging his instructions needlessly and that Laila was flirting when she smiled at him.

Why was Ora oblivious to this, when her eyes were eagle sharp to see that he and the other Arab boys were kept apart from Laila and Ayesha? At last night's folk dancing, he had paired off with Laila, and very adroitly Ora moved her away from the position opposite him to the end of the line. He had seen Laila more often when they were in their own village.

He was getting fed up with the *kibbutz*. Why was he doing such menial work? What was he trying to prove? He kept asking himself questions, and the answer—to be with Laila—was no longer valid. They saw very little of each other. Abdul had said, when he told him of the project, "Wonderful! You'll be useful to us yet!" but right now he did not want to be of use to anyone; he wanted to be in his little red racer that leaped over roads as if it were winged.

Why did he always have to defer to the wishes of others so that he could feel himself to be one of them? He thrust the spade into the earth and jabbed away as if he were attacking an enemy.

Watching Fared at the last of the saucers, Ora thought he was making the earth fly as if to rid himself of some demon. In the row next to him, Adnan was keeping pace with the others, but she detected a twitch of pain across his face. To question him now would only embarrass him, she knew.

Now the pipes were all put in place and water sprouted into the saucers, and the little saplings stood upright in neat and even rows. She left the field to chat with Amitai, who was on the upper level where cattle were grazing. He had been disagreeable since the decision was made to put the lower field to fruit, instead of leaving it as a pasture for the herd.

She saw him riding away toward the eastern fence, to where the Syrian mountains rose skyward with a scatter of small white boxes, which were Arab houses clinging to the hillside. She felt certain that Amitai had seen her. He was annoyed with her because she had voted against him on the matter of the field.

The cattle were grazing leisurely over the wide expanse of the higher hill. They were the Hereford crossbreed that were raised for meat and, until recently, had provided a sizable income for the *kibbutz*. Ora saw in their diminished numbers the pain that Amitai experienced when he saw them each morning. Four years ago there had been 300 in his herd. Then, one night, the Syrians cut a section of the fence and led off thirty cows. The *kibbutz* had to ransom them back. Several years ago, the Arabs knifed two guards and made off with twenty more cows. Then Amitai built himself a shed there and spent the nights in it, with his rifle at a hand's distance. There was no more rustling until a few months ago, when he was awakened by sounds of movement in the grass. The infiltrators were dark humps moving in the shadow of the light cast by the bulb atop the fence and, while his volley of shots alerted the members below, they had not come fast enough to avert a calamity. The Syrians had slaughtered eighteen cows.

From where Ora stood she could clearly see the Syrian village where, about six years ago, there had been fraternization between Arab and Jewish farmers, and she thought then that surely peace between them was more than a hope—that the fire in the Syrian wheatfields they had helped to extinguish would also snuff out the enmity that existed.

When the smoke from the Syrian village billowed out, the *kibbutz* members had scrambled up the Syrian hillside with fire-fighting equipment, and the Syrian army officer, with a map of the minefield that separated the two villages, had guided them safely upward. There had been rejoicing when the fire was finally under control. Syrians and Israelis had embraced; good wishes and promises to visit each other had been exchanged; but now. . . .

Now the Syrian wheatfields were plowed under and she could see that the clefts in the eroded, tawny hills were trenches and dugouts. If she had her field glasses as she had the other day she would see the gun muzzles staring down at them from their topmost hill. In the range of these guns and pinpointing them were the fields and buildings of her *kibbutz* as well as of the neighboring one. She turned away and saw in the field below her that all the saplings were in place and that the youths were now tamping down the soil around them.

Waving his hat, Amitai galloped toward Ora, and she waved back. She felt good about his greeting; it was a sort of admission, a subtle yielding, that the members had been right in voting to make use of the lower field. It had lain fallow for three years, and there was no hope of increasing Amitai's herd while the war clouds were darkening. He came swinging his rope so that the loop became circles whirling in the air. He reined in his horse and leaped off it, landing firmly on his feet. Ora laughed at this bit of theatrics. Amitai was passionately devoted to American westerns, which were frequently shown in the *kibbutz,* despite the groans of "not another western!"

His craggy face eased into a smile. "And how are all your little Arabs today?" he asked with friendly sarcasm.

"They're a good bunch. They pull their weight," she said.

"*Beseder.* Okay. For now. But later, for whom will they pull their weight—when the war comes?"

"*If,* not when," she replied.

In the newly planted field the trucks were filling up for the return drive. Fared, who was in the last one, rose when Ora came running down the hill, and he leaned forward to give her a hand. She felt that the gesture reinforced her answer to Amitai.

6

Fared Dodges a Problem

When the Tabari truck let Fared off at the foot of his private road, he paused a moment to relish the beauty of his house and the pleasure of homecoming. Set high above the road, the tall-windowed stone house, with its slender fluted columns, looked flattened against the steep hillside. There were two levels to the house, each supporting a terrace that led to a connecting section. Their *diwan* stood slightly to the rear, and was almost covered by the low-hanging branches of an ancient fig tree. A rock fence enclosed the expansive grounds on three sides.

His father stood waiting on the terrace and embraced him with a cry of *"Ah'lan Wasaha' ilan!"* Fared asked after his grandfather's health.

"He will live! *Inshallah!* Today he was out of bed five times for his prayers."

Inside, the living room—with its rose-colored, damask-covered walls, the red velvet drapes, the small gilt chairs at each window, the brocaded chairs grouped around the low, copper tables, the rugs on the mosaic floor—struck Fared, after the simple *kibbutz* furniture, as rather ornate but cozy.

Somewhere in the house, a gramophone was playing an American rock record. Before Fared could ask about his mother and sisters, they came into the room with cries of welcome and embraced him, all speaking at once and asking the same questions as to how he had fared at the *kibbutz.*

"Enough now!" Khalil said, with an impatient clap of his hands at his daughters. Promptly, but reluctantly, they released him and left the room, while the mother lingered, urging him to come, after he had seen his grandfather, for the delicacies he loved to eat.

Taking Fared's arm, Khalil led him along a wide hall to the grandfather's room. "I will leave you alone with him."

Wrapped in a blanket, his grandfather sat in a tall armchair and, at first, Fared saw only the white mane of hair under the black skullcap. He seemed to have shriveled since Fared had seen him last. He was fingering his beads, and Fared waited at the door for the whisper of prayer to cease. When it did, he moved closer and said, "May your prayers find favor with Allah!" He took his grandfather's hand and kissed it.

"May His blessings be upon you," Abu Sa'id responded. Inside the white frame of beard, the hawklike face was the color of wax, and only the beaked nose and the shaggy black eyebrows gave it a measure of the strength it once possessed. The questioning thrust of Abu Sa'id's shrewd eyes alerted Fared that he might be in for an accounting of himself.

Instead, Abu Sa'id chuckled. "Everyone here goes about with the look of a mourner. On your face, it is not natural."

"You should know this is my look when I am serious. Not natural." Fared's tension eased when the old man laughed. "Besides, Dr. Erni told me there is no cause for mourning." As he spoke, he brought a chair and sat down. The grandfather reached for his hand, and Fared was surprised at the strength in the grip of the clawlike fingers.

Abu Sa'id's face softened with the whimsical smile as he said, "Once, in the time of the British when they searched for guns in Noah's old *kibbutz* in the Jezreel, and he was shot, he said to me, 'Death is a necessary end but why now when I still have so much to do!' Yes, I have much to do yet—may Allah grant me the days. Now tell me how it was in the *kibbutz.*"

"Everything is too organized, but they work very hard. They live much better than our *fellaheen.*"

"That is because they work very hard. They plan, and they all pull together."

"But that is socialism up there. Would you want it for our *fellaheen?*"

"If they can have their rights and live better and with security in old age, yes."

Surprised, Fared raised an eyebrow. His grandfather, a very rich man, was advocating socialism!

As if sensing his thoughts, Abu Sa'id went on, but now his voice was harsh. "But not the kind of socialism they have in Russia—or what Nasser calls socialism."

Fared felt uneasy at the turn in their talk. Before his illness, his grandfather and he had differed in their opinion of Nasser. In the awkward silence that followed, Abu Sa'id gave a snort on some inward thought.

"In the *kibbutz* they think there will be war," Fared offered. "They don't talk about it, but they're digging shelters."

There was no reply. His grandfather's head drooped, his eyelids lowered and his hand in Fared's loosened its grip. Fared was about to ease his hand away when Abu Sa'id's eyes opened and his voice spoke with the cutting edge of anger. "Every day that *shaitan* in Cairo threatens that his army will sweep the Jews into the sea. The Egyptians couldn't do it before, nor will they now. Nasser should remember our proverb: He who sows thorns will not harvest grapes, and he who lights a fire may be burned."

He was in for it now, Fared knew. His grandfather's contempt for the Egyptians began during the First World War, when he and Noah had been in the British prison camps in Egypt.

"The Egyptian never was a soldier," he continued, "he never rose against his conquerors. For over a thousand years Egypt was a land in captivity. How, then, will they drive the Jews into the sea? Tell me that."

"With Russian arms, my grandfather—the most superior in the world. More advanced than the

American. This I heard many times over the radio."

"But will the Russians do their fighting for them?"

"But it is a different Egypt now. They've made a revolution; it brought changes."

"Revolutions do not always bring freedom. And do not mistake changes for progress."

"True, my grandfather, but there are improvements." He fell silent when he saw his grandfather nodding sleepily, his eyes half-closed. Then, with a jerk, the old head fell back, and the deathly pallor of the face frightened Fared. Should he tell his father to phone Dr. Erni to come at once?

His grandfather stirred and muttered something sleepily, and his head moved back into position. Slowly Fared eased his hand free and, rising noiselessly, lifted him and carried him to his bed. As he tucked the blanket around him, Abu Sa'id sighed with relief.

Fared sat down beside him and brooded on what life would be like without his grandfather. The thought of it was like a sudden weight on his heart. He had always felt his love a strength inside him. There had never been the bond of shared words and camaraderie with his own father as there had been with his grandfather.

Fared was just dozing off when he heard footsteps and then, softly, his father came into the room, wearing his nightgown and carrying a pallet.

"I will stay with him," he whispered as he spread the thin straw mattress on the floor, alongside the bed. "You can leave now."

It took only a minute for Fared to bolt the house,

and another to get into his car and start it. He drove as if to outrace the high wind and returned several hours later, when he was too groggy with fatigue to spin the car safely around the sharp turns in the hilly roads.

He woke late the next morning and lay in bed enjoying its spacious comfort as well as the thought that tomorrow, too, he could rise late, and that for two full days there would be neither classes nor work of any kind. Quietly the door opened and his mother's round, good-natured face came around it. He feigned sleep. She closed the door. Then, one by one, his three sisters looked in until there was nothing to do but rise, wash and dress for breakfast—which was a feast of all the edibles he loved.

It was past noon when he went to his grandfather's room. He heard his father's voice, sounding defensive against the querulous voice of the older man. Listening, Fared knew that his father was reporting on his investments. He opened the door slightly, and his father turned and frowned. "We are busy. I will let you know when we are finished."

He decided to take his car and drive to Laila's house under the pretense of visiting Adnan. One way or another, he would let Laila know he would be waiting for her at the Tomb of the Holy Man. He was just about to get into his car when he felt a stinging slap on his back. Turning, he saw his former classmate, Abdul Yunis, who grinned as if he had won a point. Fared had always bested him on the sports field, but Abdul always came out top man in class while he, Fared, limped in far behind.

Short and wiry, with a thick-haired, massive head, Abdul's dark, compelling eyes had a way of holding one riveted to him and then, with a mocking smile, making one feel foolish, as he did Fared now. Although he did not fear Abdul physically, and could beat him to a pulp if the need ever arose, Fared disliked and yet admired him for his superior intelligence, his daring and his tricky resourcefulness.

At the last political election in the village, it was Abdul who schemed to fill the voter envelopes with pictures of Nasser. Abdul never revealed how he had contrived to get the envelopes, but some of his versions of his daring amused Fared as he helped to insert the pictures inside. The conspiratorial work established a bond between them. And then, yielding to Abdul's urging, which he immediately regretted, he joined the Communist party, which he knew his grandfather detested. It was a secret he kept from his grandfather as well as from Laila, and he pondered on how to extricate himself without arousing Abdul's contempt.

"You haven't been to our last two meetings," Abdul said amiably. "What kept you away?"

"How could I? My grandfather's illness—and last week I spent at the *kibbutz*. I told you I would."

"What is it like there?"

"It's all right for Jews but not for us," Fared replied, thinking of what to say that would please Abdul, and yet not be disparaging of the *kibbutz*. "They've lost a lot of cattle, so they've turned the field into an apple orchard."

"The cow pasture?"

"No, the one just below." Fared wondered how

Abdul knew that the cows were pastured on the old topmost field.

"Are there many soldiers up there?"

"Soldiers? I didn't see any. Some of the younger men, the eighteen-year-olds, are leaving for the army."

"If no soldiers are there, how are they manning the gun emplacements?"

"I didn't see any."

"But they must be preparing for war—or aren't you allowed to move around freely?"

"Of course I'm allowed!"

"They must be stocking their arsenal."

"I'm kept too busy to notice."

"Well, begin noticing. And find out where the generator is, as well."

Just then his father called from the terrace and, with an abrupt nod at Abdul, Fared loped up to the house. He had given Abdul only unimportant information, but he felt uneasy about it, nevertheless.

Before he came into his room, he heard his grandfather's voice in all its old vigor. His mother's face was crumpled with weeping, and she kept wringing her hands nervously.

"I want meat on my plate!" the old man growled. "I still have teeth! This is for infants!"

Placatingly, Fared said, "But, my grandfather, Dr. Erni told her to prepare the food like this."

"Then let him eat it," he said and pushed aside the plate.

Fared's mother took away the heavy pot and plate, wiped the small inlaid table with a towel, and sighed heavily when Fared opened the door for her and gave her a commiserating smile.

"Fared! Sit down!" His grandfather's voice was stern, but it was not until he saw his face that Fared became tense. He cursed Abdul. If he hadn't come, Fared would now be with Laila and be spared his grandfather's bad humor. Whatever it was that troubled him must have to do with his father's inept handling of his business affairs. The mess for his meal had further exasperated him, Fared thought, and waited for him to speak.

"Was that Abdul with you outside?"

"Yes, my grandfather. He knew I would be home today."

"It is said that it was Abdul who stuffed the election envelopes with Nasser's pictures."

Fared's heart began to pound, and his mouth went dry. He said, "I heard this, too."

"Also, it is known that he is a Communist."

Fared managed to look surprised.

"It is allowable in Israel but not in the Arab countries. And so we have two cancers here, the one that bows to Moscow has elected four deputies of their party to the Knesset, and the one that bows to Peking."

"But if it is allowable. . . ."

"It is best that you do not see Abdul."

"But he is of our *hamula!*" Now he did not have to feign surprise.

"There are some who bring no honor to us. Now help me to bed. In my own house I hunger, and food is denied me."

Later that day, as he set out for Laila's home, he felt immense relief that his grandfather had not pressed him with questions, as he would have admitted everything. He thought now that there was no longer a reason to tell his grandfather, since he was resolved to break with Abdul. Nevertheless, he felt burdened with guilt, and, for the rest of the holiday, he dreaded the visits to his grandfather.

When he set out for the *kibbutz* truck, early Sunday morning, he felt as if he had been reprieved.

Laila and Ayesha were already waiting at the clinic collection point. Ayesha was telling her something, and Laila was listening intently. When she saw him, her face came alight with love, and he ached to seize her in his arms. All at once his burden dissolved, and he said lightheartedly, "Did your brother tell you I dropped in to see Adnan?"

Laughing, she said, "My parents took me visiting, but my brothers thought it odd that you came for Adnan and didn't know that he was staying over at the *kibbutz* for their *Purim* Festival."

"I'd forgotten," he said, and she gave him a look that was almost coy in its hidden laughter.

7

The Classroom and the Campfire

Whenever Laila entered Ora's class, she quickened with anticipation that something new and interesting was about to unfold. Ora was a born teacher; when the occasion warranted it, she spoke brusquely with the voice of authority, but in the classroom she was a friend among friends.

Fared and the other boys of their group were already in their seats when Laila came in with Ayesha. Yawning, Fared nodded sleepily at her. The room buzzed with talk of the campfire that would be held that night, but the chatter subsided when Ora appeared and began with a brief account of the early Jewish pioneer settlements which had been aided by the World Zionist Organization.

"Zionism as a world movement did not come into existence until the urgency of events created the need for it—the persecution of Jews in tsarist Russia-Poland and, later, in Hitler's Germany. The organization raised funds to buy land in Palestine on which to settle Russian-Polish Jews who were subjected to massacres, directed by the tsars forced to live in ghettos, denied civil rights and the protection of the law.

"The British government was in sympathy with the aims of this movement and, on November 2, 1917, issued the Balfour Declaration to support the establishment in Palestine of a national home for the Jewish people, on land bought by Jews.

"The League of Nations approved the Declaration, as did the Arab leaders whose countries had been liberated from Ottoman rule by the Allied victory that ended the First World War. These Arab leaders publicly stated that Jewish immigration would contribute to the development and progress of the Middle East.

"This, I admit, is instant history," Ora said, "and now I come to the history that is immediate and relevant to you—the *kibbutz* movement. The pioneers came here with a twofold purpose—to rebuild the homeland, as tillers of the soil, and thereby rebuild themselves. They found a barren, impoverished, sparsely populated land and, as had the Arabs, hired themselves as laborers on the farms and vineyards of the earlier Jewish settlers. But soon they found that this was not what they had come for. The exploitation of labor was against their ideals. They resolved to seek a new, communal way of life in which land would be bought and held in common, and all would share in the work and responsibilities as well as the achievements. Thus, the first *kibbutz*—

Degania—struggled into existence to give reality to these ideals.

"The word *kibbutz* means a group—or a 'gathering-in.' *Kibbutz* is an enlarged family; it is group living in a rural community, based on a system of collective ownership of all property. The land is worked by all, for the benefit of all its members, for the common good instead of for individual profit. Members work in return for their housing, food, clothing, health services, social and educational benefits and maintenance in old age. The *kibbutz* aims—and succeeds at—raising living standards as well as the cultural and educational standards of all its members. It is constructive idealism at work—and it is succeeding.

". . . Now, before I go more comprehensively into the *kibbutz* movement, are there any questions?"

The Arab students were still writing notes, but one of them asked, "If they were so poor when they came, how did they get the money to buy land, tools and the means to survive while they were building the *kibbutz*?"

"A very good question," Ora said and smiled. "From the Jewish National Fund, a worldwide organization formed for this specific purpose. And we paid dearly for every *dunim* we bought. The land was under rocks or swamps, land that had been untilled for many hundreds of years, and we brought this barren wasteland back to fruitfulness. We worked it into a green reality."

Now Laila raised her hand. "Would you recommend this communal system for Arabs?"

"Why not! The government encourages it and has already provided Arab farmers who pool their lands with loans, farming machinery and technical knowhow. People from Asian and African countries come here to study the *kibbutzim,* and return home to put this system to work for them. But we do not impose our way of life on anyone, neither Jew nor Arab."

"But we Arabs are too individualistic for that way of life," Fared said. "Surely there must be a loss of one's self, one's individualism in such group living."

"The pioneers who came were individualists— they were students and teachers and philosophers and workers. For them, group living must have been a real test—their beginnings were in flimsy tents or huts so crowded that they lived within each other's breath. Now our members live in spacious cottages, our schools train children to think independently, and this is true mind-development. Our cultural clubs help our members to realize themselves creatively, and this builds individualism."

As she spoke, she noticed the skeptical smile twisting Adam's lips, as if what she said was contrary to the facts and his experience, as if everything she had said was only for the gullible ones.

"Adam, how would you compare our collectives with those of the Polish, as to incentive and living standards?"

Slowly he rose. He had an odd way of rising; his long, stringy body unfolded slowly, as if reluctant to support the effort.

"Your question is irrelevant because you do not

have socialism here. Real socialism cannot be built within a capitalist society such as Israel is."

There were hoots from some of the pupils, and Ora made a gesture for them to cease. "Socialism, Adam, is collective ownership of property and means of production. We enforce the socialist principle of 'from each according to his ability, to each according to his needs.' And, equally important, we have the right to openly protest—and vote for changes. We do not use hired labor or profit from the labor of outsiders."

"That is not so!" Adam countered. "There are Arabs who work for wages here."

"Only on construction of buildings, but not in production, not in the fields."

"When I came here, I saw Arabs working in the fields and in the machine shop. That is production!" Adam said.

"They were being taught and trained to operate farm machinery. The Tabaris, brothers of Laila and Adnan, were among them, and now they have organized a machine cooperative in Umm Tubas. Any more questions?"

There were none. There was to be a campfire that night, and everyone remembered they had chores before attending it.

Aviva waited outside the library for Laila and Ayesha, who were inside selecting books to take home for their Sabbath tomorrow. They were to help her get the food for the *kumsitz* from the commissary.

The library stood at an angle from the dining

hall, and the people going down the ramps at either end greeted Aviva in passing. They were going to see an English film. The dining hall was aglitter with lights, and she could see her mother, Noah and Avram at their usual window table. Erni stood talking to them, and Aviva wondered if he was about to sit down to eat, or had already finished his meal. She knew by his white jacket that he hadn't left the Umm Tubas clinic in time to change for his meal. At breakfast this morning she had asked him to come to the *kumsitz,* and he had professed to be shocked.

"A youth campfire? At my age?"

"Why not? You're no ancient! Come!"

Would he?

In the rear room of the library building that contained the rock and classical collection, a Beatles record was throbbing plaintive sounds into the air and, above it, she heard a rhythmic thumping. Must be Yoram, she thought. He fancied himself a drummer, and this was his last chance to play with the Beatles before he went into the army tomorrow.

She began a slow, swaying dance, elbows bent as she had seen in American films, when she was seized and whirled about. Erni.

"That's the way we danced when I was your age," he said, loosening his hold on her. She felt her face burning with the excitement of being in his arms. "No dancing apart as you do now—alienation dancing I call it, moving as if in a trance. When we danced, we covered ground."

"That, Father Time, was because you thought there was no tomorrow. But we know there is," she said and glided away, rippling her arms and spinning into an arabesque. "There now, is this more to your taste?" she asked, laughing.

"Much more," he said.

"Coming to the campfire?"

"It's possible," he said and started up the path toward his cottage. He stopped, turned back, and said, "Vivi, at the dancing tonight, pull Adam into it."

"Ugh! He's stiff as iron."

"Metal is malleable," he said, and gave her ear a tug. She lunged at him with both fists and, laughing, he ducked away.

She loved the manly sound of his laughter; loved the springy yet firm way he walked; loved it that he was so handsome and yet not vain. She sighed unhappily at the thought that in six months she would be going into the army. Would he marry while she was away?

If he did marry, she would go to New York to study ballet after her army service. But would the army, with its strict discipline and hard training, grind out of her all desire for a career? What with all the threats from across the borders, she felt that a career was not only irrelevant but even vain and self-seeking. Even Moshe had ceased to talk about the school where he would study composition. The truth was in her father's letter: "The last thing Israel needs is another ballet dancer!" Was there nothing else to look forward to but a continuing struggle with the Arabs, while all the art forms withered away?

She had just said to Erni that today's kids had what his generation hadn't had—time. But had they? It all seemed so futile. Just then she saw Laila and Ayesha coming out of the library with their books, and suddenly her spirits lifted at a thought: If it is possible to be so friendly with your Arab neighbors, surely it must be possible to live in amity with those across the borders!

"They usually have their campfires on Friday nights, but tomorrow Yoram and a few boys are going into the army," Adam offered, as he led Fared and Adnan to the field where it was being held. They saw lights flickering through the trees, and this, as well as Moshe's harmonica playing, guided them to the fire.

A quick glance at the youths told Fared that the other three of his group had decided to come after all. They sat next to their roommates, munching sunflower seeds from a common plate.

Several girls stood watching Yoram as he started to build the fire. "I could use more branches," he said, and the girls set out looking for them. One of the boys came to play Yoram's accordion that lay on the ground. "Your hands clean?" Yoram asked. "Last time I had to scrub the keys." The boy muttered something as his fingers ran an arpeggio over the keys.

Fared watched two boys wrestling and considered taking on the winner, but just then Moshe started a lively tune on his harmonica, the accordion took it up and the wrestlers broke away from each other to dance with the girls.

Neither Laila nor Ayesha were here yet, and Fared was irked. For once Ora's watchful eyes would not be on them, and he wanted to sit with Laila, apart from the others. In the three weeks they had been here, he had not once been alone with her.

Shouts of welcome greeted Aviva when she and a few girls appeared with paper sacks of food and a tray of small china cups. They were followed by two youths who carried platters of meat, which they handed to Yoram.

"Moshe, get water!" Yoram called over his shoulder. Moshe continued playing on his harmonica. "Get cracking!" Yoram ordered. Moshe calmly wiped the spittle from his harmonica and, pretending outrage, he shouted back, "He gives orders like already he's an *aluf* in the army!"

Yoram kicked him lightly to speed him along and Moshe, who considered this a gesture of affection, grinned as he picked up the pails and, rhythmically clanking them together, set off.

The noise annoyed Adam, who was sitting nearby. He thought the boy a snot-nosed brat, whom the old ones pampered because he was an orphan. He was insolent and a nuisance with his harmonica, which hung like an extension from his lips. He was Aviva's pet and anyone had to answer to her for an offense to him. Adam had enough time to swing his long legs out of Moshe's way, but he didn't. Moshe stumbled over them, dropping pails, eyeglasses and harmonica. Aviva sprang to his aid while Adnan picked up his things.

"Moshele, are you hurt?" she asked, as she yanked him to his feet. He looked at her with naked adoration and stammered, "I—you—in the firelight you looked like—like a fairy!"

"Moshe! Get cracking!" Yoram thundered out and, seizing the two pails, the boy scrambled away.

More girls came, and Fared saw Laila detach herself from them and look around. He waved, and she picked her way around the groups to reach him. She wore a sweater over a blouse and skirt, and this pleased him: She had taken his sarcastic remark about shorts seriously. She was smiling as she approached, and he thought it altogether another face, as if a light had flashed on inside, making her blue eyes as luminous as sapphires.

He cleared a space of pebbles and leaves, and they sat down, with a fence of cypress trees behind them. Adnan and Adam joined them but Fared's annoyed look was lost on them.

"What made you so late, Laila?" Fared asked.

"I went for a book. Fared, have you been to the library?" and added, when he shook his head, "They've hundreds of books in many languages—and . I found more than a dozen on Islamic literature! And the Persian poets were beautifully illustrated."

"In Arabic?" Adnan asked.

"There were several, but most were in Hebrew and English."

Moshe brought the filled pails to Yoram and then began playing a tune that was sweetly haunting. Fared slipped his arm around Laila. She looked up at him and pressed her lips against his cheeks. The pale sky arching overhead was cloudless, with a scatter of stars that shone brilliantly. Rustled by the wind, the leaves made a whispering accompaniment to Moshe's sad song. Laila sighed with utmost content as she settled deeper into Fared's arms.

Several boys were tumbling and Yoram, with a wild yell, went sailing over the fire. Adam tittered.

"Hey! Yoram, if you had lifted your behind like that yesterday, we'd have won the game!" one of the boys hooted.

Adam rose and made a running jump over the fire, and Aviva said, "With practice, you could qualify for the Olympics!"

Rising, Fared helped Laila to her feet to move closer to the fire. Now Moshe, chest outthrust and with elbows sawing the air as he ran forward, went flying over the coals and landed on Adam's foot. Adam hissed out a Polish oath that wiped the elated grin from Moshe's face, and he stammered an apology.

"Adam, he didn't do it on purpose!" Aviva snapped out and hooked her arm around Moshe.

The girls came to the fire to watch as several youths vaulted over the agitated coals. Their cheers roused others to take the hurdle, when Yoram yelled, "Cut it out! You're fanning the coals," but stopped when they moved aside for Fared.

Laila watched as his lithe figure leaped with ease and grace high over the fire. There were murmurs of "ohs" from the girls, and Adam gave him an approving slap on his back.

Yoram went back to tending the fire. The coals were now too hot for the meat, and he turned away to watch the boys forming a human pyramid as they mounted each other's backs with agility. Moshe, the short one in the group, stood grinning at its top. One by one they tumbled down, and Yoram turned back to the fire, which was settling into a mass of hot white ashes. He poured water into two coffee pots, which he set over the fire, and then speared the chunks of meat on skewers for grilling.

Presently, the tantalizing odor of meat sizzling over coals rose in the air, and the lids of the two coffee pots began a rhythmic hopping.

With a small spoon Aviva began measuring sugar into the cups. "Counting the grains, Vivi?" someone called out.

"Don't be stingy. Sugar isn't gold!" said another.

"Tell that to Chaika," Aviva retorted. "She doles it out now as if it were her blood."

Squeals broke out as fingers touched the charred meat. Fared picked up a long twig and skewered a piece for Laila.

"Now that's a true gentleman—not like the wolves here," Aviva said, as she sat down beside Ayesha, blowing at the meat that she tossed from palm to palm.

"Anything left for the aged?"

"Erni!" Aviva screamed out and stood up to wave him over.

A girl handed him a small cup of coffee. He sipped, and said, "Good coffee!" He started to move toward Aviva, when Yoram held out a square of meat on the end of his big fork. "Nearly raw, Erni, exactly as you like it."

Biting into it, Erni said, "For rubber it's not bad at all," and, chewing, he wound his way to Aviva and sat down beside her.

Now a moving circle of light pierced the hill road, and a fluff of white hair, over a round face, could be seen in its ambience. *"Shalom, chaverim!"* a hearty voice called out.

"Noah! Sit here!" "Sit by me, Noah!" voices called out. *"Sabba,* I'm near the trees!" rose urgingly. As he moved forward, Noah ruffled a head here, tweaked a nose there and, with his searchlight, picked out Adnan. Reaching him, Noah lowered himself beside Adnan.

The boy's face came alight with pleasure. The *mukhtar* of the *kibbutz,* known and respected by the Arabs in the entire region, whom they called on to mediate their quarrels, had sought him out to sit beside him!

"Chaverim!" Noah began, and the talk began to subside as always when the old *vattik,* the founder of the *kibbutz,* spoke. He was no windy orator like the others but always spoke to the point, and briefly. He said, "I have a gift for you—a poem!"

"That's a gift?" Yoram's voice went high with indignation.

". . . more precious than money," Noah went on.

"I'll take money!" Yoram retorted.

"Ignoramus! Beatnik! Listen and enjoy! It is a poem from the heart of our friend here, Adnan Tabari," he said and unfolded a paper, his searchlight focusing on the words.

The Bridge

A bridge is arms outspread and a welcoming
Across it a coming and going of brother peoples
To stir our Land into a hopeful new dawn,
And build the good life, a glory to mankind.

*The light of Moses illumined Mohamet
And the seed of Abraham begot us.
Take my hand, brother Jew, and clutch it tight
So that none can sever what is cemented with love.*

*Together we will strive for our Homeland.
We will sing in the harmony that is unity
And lo! the world shall praise
The ways of peace of our twin nations!*

"There is more," Noah said as he folded the paper and put it into his pocket. "Ora hadn't time to translate the rest. You will hear the entire poem at the *Seder* festival at Passover."

Applause broke out and Adnan, who had not altogether understood the Hebrew translation, sensed that they liked it, by the silence during the reading and the shouts of "*Tov*, Adnan!"

Lightly fingering his accordion, Yoram said, "For poetry it isn't bad—if you like poetry. Me, I prefer dancing!" And, striking up a gay Israeli tune, he bounced to his feet. Aviva thought that when Yoram moved, his stocky body seemed earthbound, yet he was airborne when he danced. She leaped up, seized Erni's arm and pulled him up, then tugged at Adam's. All at once there was a circle of dancers, arms laced around shoulders, stamping out a *hora* beat and roaring out the song. Now Laila and Fared were pulled into the ring, and Noah, clutching Adnan's arm, hopped with him into the circle.

Old Noah hopped into the middle of the smaller circle and stomped out a dance by himself, the white plume of hair tossing wildly. Then, suddenly he said, "Enough!" and, slipping through the two rings, left for the cottages below. As if at a signal, Fared and the four Arabs, arms around shoulders, leaped as one into a *debka,* handkerchiefs fluttering at each end of the line.

Suddenly thunder growled. The dancing stopped, and Aviva stood transfixed.

War! The Syrians were firing!

Erni spoke to several youths, and they hurried away. Now the thunder rolled away into silence.

A nervous shudder went through Aviva. Was it beginning? Fear took hold of her, and she wanted to run. "I must not—I will not be a coward!" She took a slow, deep breath and held it as her eyes sought out Erni. Seeing him, she released her breath. He was standing with the Arab boys and quietly talking to them. She came toward him, and he asked, "Leaving already?"

"N-no!" her voice wavered, and, with a toss of her head, she added indignantly, "Of course not!" Then, as if she had come expressly to do this, she scooped up a few handfuls of earth and threw them on the fire. She felt calm now, and joined the group around Erni.

They talked in low voices. The dying embers threw a lemony glow over their faces, and Erni's pipe wafted a sweet aroma into the air.

Fared, his fingers laced with Laila's, whispered, "Maybe the *hamula* will meet tomorrow, and my grandfather will bring up the matter of our marriage."

"But what if they decide against us?" said Laila.

"Then we will plan what to do. They should not have the right to decide our fate for us!"

Yoram threw water on the fire, and a cloud of steam hissed up. The gold-streaked coals glowed an instant and then blackened.

"It was a good *kumsitz*," Aviva said when Erni took her arm and they began walking to the downward road.

"Yes, it was," he agreed, sensing a lack of conviction by her choice of words. Never a moderate in expressing herself, Aviva was given to the use of superlatives; good was almost a negative to her. The earlier panic he had seen in her eyes was gone, and she was her lively self again, teasing Yoram about drenching his hair with Fared's lotion. "The army will have to disinfect you before they let you join the men."

They all laughed, and the echo of it was a reassuring sound to her. Erni slipped his arm around her waist, and she covered his hand with hers as they walked to the dwellings below.

8

Silence Means Consent

That Sunday morning, as usual, Laila and Adnan were the first to appear at the collection point in Umm Tubas, each with a book to be returned to the *kibbutz* library. Ora always arrived promptly at seven o'clock, but there was no sign of her truck on the empty village road. They could see Ayesha turning into the main street from the mosque section where she lived. She wore her hair in a ponytail, as did Aviva and the girls in the *kibbutz*. It tossed from side to side as she jogged along, a book tucked under her arm. Both girls wore the blue, thimble-shaped canvas hats worn by the *kibbutz* members.

"Ora not here yet?" Ayesha asked in surprise.

"Maybe she stopped to pick up supplies," Adnan offered.

"She usually does, but even so she gets here by

seven," Laila said, and bit her lower lip on a premonition of disaster—Ora had met with an accident . . .
something had gone wrong at the *kibbutz*. Usually a
premonition came to her with a freezing sensation,
but it didn't now because, at that moment, she saw
Fared and the three boys of the group striding down
the hill road. He seemed in good spirits, and this,
Laila thought, was a departure from his usual sullen
mood in the rising hour at the *kibbutz*. He approached, smiling at her, and she thought he seemed
more confident, as if what he had resolved at the
kumsitz had bolstered him, given him real self-assur-
ance, instead of the pose of one he usually assumed.

"Where's Ora?" he asked. Usually he came late,
delaying them, and this morning he wanted to prove
by his promptness his newly acquired sense of
responsibility.

But for the hammering and clanging of metal on
metal in the machine shop farther up the street, the
village lay quietly enfolded in the mist of early
morning. A flock of birds pecked away on the
vegetable patch that fronted the grade school
grounds, and a dog barked a warning at them. The
birds scattered to safety on the branches of a tree.
On the terraces of the two coffee shops, the stools
and small tables had not yet been set out, and the
provision shop was still shuttered.

Fared glanced at his watch; seven-thirty.

"I will telephone," Laila said, and started for the
machine shop when she saw a moving vehicle at the
far end of the village road, and she cried out with
relief, "There's Ora!"

When Ora drew up and braked, Fared said, "We thought you'd forgotten us."

"Not likely." Ora smiled, but Laila thought it was not her usual smile but a forced one. Something was wrong, surely.

"Let's get going," Ora said, and the boys climbed onto the rear while the girls got into the cab of the truck.

Ora swung around, in such a sharp curve, that she almost struck the electric pole, and righted herself with a jolt that nearly flung the two girls against the windshield. It was so unlike Ora's smooth driving that Laila felt convinced that something was wrong.

They rode along in silence for a few minutes, and then Ora asked, "Enjoy your Sabbath?"

"Oh, yes!" Ayesha replied.

Laila tried to keep the apprehension from her voice as she asked, "Is everything all right at the *kibbutz?*"

A petrol truck came roaring down the middle of the road and Ora swerved to the side, then gave a few angry thwacks on the horn to tell the driver off. She drove on and, when she failed to reply, Laila thought she hadn't heard her question.

"No, not everything," Ora finally said. "This morning we found the new orchard destroyed—all the saplings the volunteers had planted uprooted and crushed."

Both girls shook their heads in disbelief.

Fared asked what had happened. Laila told him and he stared at her, stunned. Abdul? A sick burn of vomit came to his throat; it was his fault—he had located the new orchard for him.

Turning into the *kibbutz,* Ora drove past the congested area where men were digging trenches, and into the orchards. She parked the truck, and the youths followed her to their field. Laila gasped, "Oh, no!" It was as if some fiend had been on a rampage; the saplings had been torn up and stomped on—they lay like green bruises on the ground.

Fared's eyes were riveted to his saplings. The twenty trees he had planted had been a work of his own creation—he had felt an odd satisfaction in their growth, had come several times to see how they fared and boasted to the others that they were rising taller, sturdier than theirs. And with pride he had told his grandfather of his share in Tel Hashava's growth. It had pleased his grandfather immensely.

He knew that Ora's eyes were fixed on him, and again he felt the burning sensation of guilt. Why was it that she stared only at *him?* He turned back and saw the stricken look on Laila's face, and he said, "We'll plant new ones." He touched her arm very lightly, but she shuddered.

Ora saw Amitai looking down at them from the grazing field. When their glances met, he gave her a cynical smile and rode off. Ora thought it a forewarning of how the others would react when word reached them of the ruined orchard.

Without Aviva it was lonely that night in their cottage, and Laila sat waiting for her on the steps of the veranda. The day had begun for her with a feeling of apprehension and was ending on the dismal sense of guilt. Aviva had not turned up in the dining hall. Was she avoiding her?

There were changes everywhere, and this added to her uneasiness. There were trenches instead of flower beds, sandbags all around the outer walls of the dining halls, the tall windows crisscrossed with tape and covered with blackout curtains. All this change over the weekend! She had the feeling when she entered the dining hall that the din of conversation subsided at once. The Arab group and the ruined orchard must have been the subject they were discussing, she felt certain. And she was certain, too, that when they resumed their talk, it was of something else, for it had a different noise level. Some of the settlers smiled at her; others merely nodded. She shrank inside herself as if she were an intruder, and unwelcome.

Then, as if sensing her uneasiness, Emmi and Noah, in passing, stopped to greet her and then sat down with her. Noah glanced at her uneaten food, and said in his teasing manner, "Eat, Laila, or your father will think we starve you here," and he lifted a forkful of potatoes to her mouth. She had giggled with relief and pleasure. Emmi rose and said that there was to be a rehearsal of the Independence Day program, and to be sure to see it. Then, for the first time, she leaned over and kissed Laila.

But she still felt that the others looked warily at her. Why hadn't she seen Aviva all that day? A dusting of stars spread a milky swath in the dark, low-hanging sky that touched the spires of the cypress trees on the upper *kibbutz* fields. At night, the flowering bushes around the cottages were present only as a sweet fragrance. Laila sat hunched over, thinking of what she had heard at home that Friday. Mahmoud Shahadi, a member of the El Khoury *hamula,* had visited, and while she and her mother were preparing refreshments in the kitchen, he related what was being said.

"Yunis said that if war comes—who will survive? Not the Jews—nor those who cooperated with them." And, recalling his words, Laila froze with fear. Her father and brothers had made light of his words, but if what Yunis said was true, they would be the first ones to be seized. And then, Fared, Adnan, herself. Abdul and his friends would point fingers.

She gave a start at the crunching sound of footsteps and saw, with a cry of relief, that it was Fared and Adnan. They sat down on the steps, one on either side of her, and she felt comforted that they had come.

"The chorus is rehearsing the Independence Day program. It sounds wonderful," Adnan said breaking the silence.

Fared said, "They moved Moshe in with Adam and me. Adam hit it off wrong with him from the start. He asked Moshe why they didn't put him in with Adnan, now that Yoram is in the army and he has the room to himself, and Moshe only shrugged. Then Adam asked if he was the watchdog for the internal police, to keep his eyes on the two of us, and Moshe got snotty, saying, 'This isn't Poland or Russia. We don't keep an eye on our people to report to the police.' "

"Good for Moshe!" Laila exclaimed.

Adnan was biting his nails, a sign, she knew, of

nervousness. Then, hesitantly, he asked her, "Did—did you—feel uncomfortable with—with them?"

"A little," she admitted.

"I felt—well—as if they looked differently at me—sort of suspicious. I wish I was home. Shouldn't we leave?"

"That would only confirm their suspicions," Laila said, after which none of them spoke, though each pursued the same thought.

Finally Laila asked, "Fared, did you see Abdul on Friday?"

He gave a start. "Yes, why do you ask? I saw him at the mosque."

"What did you talk about?"

"How could we talk! The service had begun," he said irritably. Why did she mention Abdul *now* when she hadn't for ages? She sat with her elbows propped on her knees, her hands cupping her chin, and, in an anguished voice, she said, "Ours is a destructive nationalism."

It was then that Fared felt the noose around his neck—with the other end of the rope in Abdul's hand.

The house in which Ora lived was a two-story dwelling at the far end of a lane of cottages. It had been built to accommodate African and Asian students who came to study the *kibbutz* system. When they finished their studies a few years later, other African and Asian students came, some of whom requested that they share the Israeli student dormitories. The vacant apartments were then occupied by Ora, while Emmi and Avram shared the apartment next to several students from Uganda. Erni lived on the floor above, with Amitai and his wife Malka as neighbors.

Ora's apartment had the usual *kibbutz* basic furnishings; a studio-bed, a table, several chairs and an armchair, a chest of drawers and bookshelves. Bright scatter rugs on the stone floor, colorful African masks and ebony sculptures, a richly designed, hand-woven tapestry on one wall (all gifts of departing students) gave the room a rather exotic look, but the beige spread on the couch and matching window drapes toned it all down into a harmonious blend.

In the kitchen alcove, Ora was preparing coffee which she set to boil on the electric unit, and took out the food for Aviva she had brought earlier from the *kibbutz* kitchen. At the table Aviva frowned as she read her father's letter.

"Paul is bringing that dreadful wife of his—oh, *Ima!* She makes me feel as if—as if I'm some kind of odd species she's studying."

The glass of water in Ora's hand shook, and she turned away to suppress her laughter. "Vivi, don't exaggerate," she said.

The letter Aviva was reading had been written to Ora. Paul was pessimistic about the prospect for peace and was coming immediately after the semester ended. He would take Aviva back with him. "But if conditions worsen, I want you to send Aviva . . . in fact, don't wait, send her on the first available plane. Susan wants her with us and knows a good ballet school. . . ."

Ora had agonized over the decision to keep the

letter a secret, but Erni had advised her to let Aviva see it and come to her own decision. Now, as she brought a plate of food to the table, she felt tense. Aviva's face was flushed with excitement.

"*Ima*—am I really going?"

Ora nodded. She wanted her daughter safe from Arab shelling, but she also wanted her within sight. Home.

"Yes, you are going. As soon as it can be arranged. But you are not eating."

"How can I? I'm much too excited! Oh, *im-aleh*. . . ." At the knock on the door, she flew to open it. Erni came in.

"Erni! I'm going! Really, I'm going." And then, suddenly, as if she had been struck by a powerful blow on the head, she stared at him wide-eyed and speechless. She went back to the chair and slumped into it, her hands clenched into fists.

Ora and Erni. With a stricken look, her eyes went from one to the other. What if something happened to them . . . to Noah . . . to Moshe . . . to the others . . . to all Israel? The safety of her father's home would be her shame all her life—if she went to New York now.

Ora . . . Erni. . . . Until this moment she had not been fully aware of their meaning in her life; she had absorbed their love—all the good things here— as unconsciously as she breathed. But suddenly she knew that they were as indispensable to her as life itself. She would not go to New York. Very definitely, no!

Erni questioned Ora with a look, and she moved a plate aside adroitly, leaving Paul's letter exposed.

"Vivi is excited about going to New York," she said in a matter-of-fact tone.

"I was—but I'm not going," Aviva said quietly.

"Why not?" he asked.

"Oh, don't press me," she cried, and then she added, "It's purely a matter of internal security. *Ima,* you write Paul I'm not coming."

"Wait a few days—just to make certain," Ora advised.

"I'm certain right now," Aviva said, with a finality that brooked no further discussion.

Glancing at his watch, Erni remarked, "The Independence Day rehearsal is due to start now. Moshe was already playing his sonata."

"Without me? He composed it for me to dance to!" Aviva cried, outraged. "Let's go!"

On the lawn outside the cottage Emmi, Avram and Noah sat talking over the events of the day. It was not entirely dark when Ora came out, and she could see the green lawns about her set off with splashes of flaming hibiscus. Emmi's eyes, she noted, were heavy lidded with weeping over Yoram's leaving for his army service. Avram, from whom Yoram had inherited his strong, muscular frame, had merely bid him good-bye with "Get cracking. The truck is needed back."

Avram gave Aviva's ponytail a tug when she passed him to kiss Noah.

"I'll walk you to the auditorium," Erni offered.

"For exercise—or company?" Aviva asked.

"Could be both," he said, taking her elbow and steering her away from the border of hibiscus at the lawn's edge.

When the two vanished around the curve of the lane, Ora asked, "What was it like in the dining hall? Did they talk about the orchard?"

"It was a bit sticky," Emmi replied. "The talk was—oh, well—you know . . ."

"Amitai began it at his table," Avram put in. "But they toned it down immediately when the five Arab boys came in."

"They all turned up for their classes," Ora said. "But in my class not one of them asked a question. Unusual for Laila."

"Amitai and a few others think we should disband the group," Noah said. "He insists now isn't the time for experiments."

"Nonsense!" Ora scoffed. "The other *kibbutzim* have dozens more Arab students than we have." She paused, then added, "I'd like to live in a time when all we're worried about are the normal, everyday problems of the human variety—very simple."

"Even that we'd complicate," Noah said with a chuckle. "We've a genius for doing that."

They laughed. Noah could always be relied on to say what could best help everyone over an awkward —or depressing—moment.

Laila had long since taken off the bedcovers, hers as well as Aviva's, folded them neatly over a chair, and turned on the small light in the foyer. Now she lay in bed straining for the sound of Aviva's footsteps.

Why had she not seen her all day? Was she deliberately keeping out of sight? Should they leave the *kibbutz*, as Adnan suggested? She was absorbed in her questions when the door slammed shut. Aviva never did anything quietly. Laila closed her eyes as if deeply asleep.

Aviva bent over her and tickled her. Laila sat up, feigning a startled cry.

"You weren't asleep!" Aviva said as she sat down beside her. "Your eyelashes fluttered. Oh, it's been such a hectic day!"

Laila tensed—again the ruined orchard?

"Early this morning Emmi and I took the five- and six-year-olds to the Kibbutz Shlomo pool—their teacher is in the reserves and was called back to the army. One of the kids nearly drowned; several ate like pigs and vomited; and two just took off by themselves! Emmi wasn't frantic, but I was. Then I had supper in Ora's house, and there was a letter from my father. He wants me to come to New York."

"Aviva! How wonderful!"

"Yes, but not for now." Then, dismissing the matter as if it had not caused her anguish, she said, "Next week—or the week after—when we take the kids to the pool, do you want to come along? It's really fun, and we can swim, too."

"But I don't know how," Laila admitted.

"If you can move your arms and legs, you can learn to swim. I guarantee it," Aviva assured her. Then, yawning, she kissed Laila and began preparing for bed.

Yes, it will be all right, Laila thought and, comforted, she drifted off to sleep.

9

A Gathering of the *Hamula*

It was the first Friday in May, the day of the gathering of the *hamula,* and Abu Sa'id was restless and irritable. Fared, who had gone to the mosque with his father, returned to find his grandfather slumped in his armchair, his head lowered over his beard and his glasses dangling from one ear. He woke with a start when Fared began lifting him to put him to bed. "But they are coming," he said wearily.

"Not for several hours yet," Fared assured him.

Alert now, the old man straightened in his chair and ordered Fared to read.

Fared took the Koran from its place on an ebony-framed, inlaid table and resigned himself to the task. Each time he came home, seeing the shrewd eyes questioning him, he had forestalled questions by offering to read from the Holy Book. Several hours of his two-day holiday were thus consumed, with his grandfather offering an occasional comment or interpretation.

But now Fared saw that he was being studied, and sensed that questions were mounting in that wise old head against the moment appropriate to their asking.

"*Sura* 1," the grandfather directed.

Fared groaned inwardly. *Al Fatiha*, the hymn of praise to God which ends in a petition for aid and true guidance, had, at this moment, a special significance; it was intended to expose him to himself.

His grandfather suspected that something was amiss, but would not say anything until Fared spoke first. This pattern had been set early in his boyhood, but those confessions had to do with pranks, mischievous but innocently meant, while what he had done this past year was, in his grandfather's eyes, contrary to the beliefs of a true Moslem.

During those months Fared had vacillated between his faith and unbelief, and felt uneasy about it. And, because it was required of him, he went regularly to the old mosque where on his thirteenth birthday, and after he had been circumcised, he had been confirmed into the Moslem faith.

But these past four Fridays, he had sat through the *Mullah's* sermons wondering why he had rejected his old faith for the new beliefs which had led to the sabotage in the *kibbutz* orchard.

He felt himself on trial as he began reading.

     (1) In the name of God, the Compassionate Compassioner.
     (2) Praise be to God, the Lord of the Worlds.

(3) The Compassionate Compassioner.
(4) The Sovereign of the day of judgment.
(5) Thee do we worship and of Thee do we beg assistance.
(6) Direct us in the right way.
(7) In the way of those to whom Thou has been gracious, on whom there is no wrath, and who go not astray.

His grandfather gave a deep sigh, was silent a moment, and then said, "I read this and strength comes into me, and you read it with the passion of one reading a public directory. Now read *Sura* six and seven again."

As he repeated the lines he felt that his grandfather was silently probing him. Fared's fingers laced tightly, and his nails bit into the flesh of his palms as he waited for the questions to begin. When he closed the Book and rose to put it back on its table, he stood at the window, shoulders hunched, hands clenched inside his pockets.

"Now you read it as if it meant something. Fared, you come home every Friday and you speak, but say nothing I want to hear."

"You have been very ill, my grandfather."

"Only my body is. You have talked much of things that do not matter."

"Nothing matters but your health. It is more precious to me than my own life."

"Fared, you are not altogether a fool, but now you are talking nonsense. At my age, recovery from a heart ailment is a temporary gift from Allah."

"Noah is your age and yet he recovered from a mine injury that . . ."

"Noah is entitled to a miracle. I am not," Abu

Sa'id broke in, and was about to plunge in with the first of his questions when the change in Fared's face struck him. It was misery for him to see this most beloved of his kin in the grip of some trouble and be unable to reach him.

Then, in a voice that was tender, as if he were speaking to a beloved and ailing child, he said, "Speak to me, Fared. I may lack knowledge, but I do not lack love. Come, let your heart speak."

Fared saw the eyes raised to his and the love in them implored him to accept his trust. His grandfather waved him to the chair beside him, but Fared preferred not to face him. Tonelessly, he said, "Nearly one year ago I joined the Marxists," and stopped, waiting for thunder to break over him.

Quietly Abu Sa'id said, "This I knew."

Fared wheeled about to face him, and his voice rose. "You knew and said nothing?"

"I was waiting for you to speak of it. Why did you join?"

Fared rubbed his forehead and frowned, uncertain. "It wasn't what they said that pulled me in. They were a lively bunch in Nazareth—the brightest in my school belonged—the meetings were very exciting. We were in demonstrations against the government after they blew up some Arab houses. And we demonstrated for civil rights, too."

"In the matter of blowing up the houses I do not agree with the government," Abu Sa'id admitted. "Houses commit no crimes. But in what way do you lack civil rights?"

"Well, we haven't equality of opportunity and . . ."

"Is that government policy?"

"Well, not exactly, they're crying about a depression."

"Fared, in what way do you lack civil rights?"

"In many ways. Daoud Memmi wasn't even in the village when the Israeli official was shot, but they arrested him. And they voided Mustafa's election only because he is a Communist."

"Memmi is still to be tried in court. With Mustafa, fraud was proven. And there are four Communists elected to the Knesset. Mustafa went into the villages and spoke many lies against the government, without being arrested. Could he have done this in Russia, or in the other Arab countries?"

"Yes, our Arab brothers here want improvement in their lives and that will come only when there is more money spent for human needs than for defense."

They were silent a while and Abu Sa'id began to fidget in his chair. Fared knew that unless he talked now of the sabotaged field and his role in it, the burden of guilt would remain with him. He told his grandfather about it.

Abu Sa'id smiled wryly, as if expecting nothing less of Fared's group. "Of that, Abdul is not guilty. All last week he was in the hospital in Haifa—some problem in the throat. Your father took Abdul and his father to Haifa. But the others in the group are being investigated. Yes, Fared, it is true that we need more progress in our lives. But make no mistake about the Marxists—progress does not interest them—only their long-term political ends do. They create dissension as a matter of policy. To be a Communist is to vacate your will—your selfhood. Don't squander your youth on mistakes. Now, help me to bed. I must rest before our kin arrive."

Just as Fared was about to leave the room, Abu Sa'id spoke again. "Your father told me of the daughter of Ibrahim Tabari. The family is not of our sinew, but I know him to be a man of inner worth. It is said of the daughter that she is purehearted and wise with learning. When I think that you are ready for the responsibility of marriage, I will give you my blessings. Go in peace. There is nothing you have done that cannot be forgiven."

It was as if his grandfather had, with one hand, swept away his burden and with the other dealt him a crushing blow. How could he tell this to Laila without demeaning himself in her eyes?

From the side terrace of the house, Fared saw the members of his clan arriving, some wearing striped, long, coatlike garments and *kheffiyas,* others in flowing *abayahs* over dark trousers and shirts, some in suits, and a few wearing the red fez that was no longer popular among *effendis.* His father awaited them at the open door of the *diwan,* and Fared could hear his effusive greetings.

These were the senior members of the *hamula,* the ones with money and power, Fared knew. Mostly they were old, and this, too, was discouraging. Old people clung to old traditions. They would trump up all sorts of reasons why he should marry within the *hamula*—or in another that had equal status with theirs.

Abdul was at his father's side, and for once he

was clean-shaven, his hair was combed and he was wearing his good suit, yet he still had the look of an aroused eagle. He turned and saw Fared just as his father reached Khalil and was shaking hands with him. Fared thought of going inside the house, but already Abdul was coming toward him. His throat was bandaged.

Should he hint in some way that the throat operation was a good cover-up for the operation in the *kibbutz* field? Fared wondered. Instead, he remarked dryly, "The operation was rather sudden, wasn't it?"

"Not sudden enough. My tonsils have bothered me for years," Abdul replied. Fared merely nodded and began idly watching the slow procession uphill. Abdul chuckled as he said, "I like coming to these gatherings. It's like stepping back into the Middle Ages when I listen to their talk."

"That may be true of many of them, but my grandfather is very much in the present," Fared replied, and walked briskly back into the house. Abdul frowned at his sudden brusqueness.

The *diwan* was already crowded when Fared came in with his grandfather. It was a large, square-shaped, vaulted room, furnished with rattan chairs and cushioned stools that lined the walls, braziers that flared with charcoal and, here and there, straw mats and floor cushions lay scattered. All the important matters pertaining to the *hamula* were discussed here; ceremonies such as wedding or funeral feasts were held; and here the kinsmen gathered for a social hour to gossip, to comment on the news being broadcast over the radio while listening to it.

The kinsmen had waited for Abu Sa'id to appear before sitting down, and the water pipes stood waiting for them. The rhythmic clatter of pestle and mortar rose above the subdued chatter, and the aroma of coffee being pulverized was strong in the air. No one seemed to pay attention to a voice chanting over the radio.

As the guests moved toward Abu Sa'id, someone switched off the radio. Khalil brought pillows which he placed on the seat and back of a tall armchair. Abu Sa'id stood before it, shifted his glance thoughtfully from face to face and then said, "May Allah bestow His blessings on one and all."

"Allah be praised!" came the hearty response.

When the old man sat down, a few kinsmen surrounded him and wished him health and long years and then seated themselves on chairs as close to his as possible. These were of the more immediate family, while others took seats wherever they could find them.

Abdul, sitting with Fared on mats, noticed that his grandfather, Yacoub Yunis, had very adroitly managed to slip into the chair that Khalil had vacated so as to circulate among the guests.

Yacoub Yunis, a man of overpowering physical appearance, with restless, owllike eyes, a scimitar of a nose and a thick beard first inquired after Abu Sa'id's health, and then began talking of his troubles with the Israeli courts over the land the government had expropriated some years ago.

"They have taken my honor—my land," he grieved as he beat his chest with his fist. Abu Sa'id gave him a wintry smile and said, "But the govern-ment offered to pay for those *dunims!*"

"At prices of twenty years back!" Yunis ex-claimed indignantly. "I have barely enough land to feed my family! They are making a beggar of me!"

The ancient at Abu Sa'id's right leaned over to say, "I lost sixty percent of my land to the other side of the border, but I gain more from the 2,000 *dunim* I have now than I realized on the 5,000. A matter of mechanization . . . the Tabari boys from the ma-chine cooperative and, before that, the government agronomist came to advise my sons. . . ."

In an aside to his neighbor, Yunis whispered, "If the sheep knew in advance the reason for being fattened, it would not eat." His neighbor tittered behind his hand.

Khalil was back now and Yunis made to rise but was motioned to keep the seat. He stood slightly behind his father's chair and frowned at the man who was edging his chair closer to the front. This was Anwar Shahadi, who worked with the Tabari broth-ers in the machine cooperative. He was a muscular, gray-haired man whose thick black brows met over an aquiline nose. Abu Sa'id seemed genuinely pleased to see him.

Anwar Shahadi was saying, "Of course I was for an Arab victory in '48. I am, first of all, an Arab! But after the Israelis won, I reasoned thus: Before them it was the British who ruled and before them it was the Turks—always there were masters over us. Now I am a citizen with full rights. Which of us ever had a say who should be in the government? I live much better now and, if things keep improving and there is no war . . ."

Yunis whispered to his neighbor, "They've sold their souls to the Jews," to which his neighbor replied, "The tongue has no bones. It can wag this way and that. If there is war, wait, you will see."

The talk seemed to be coursing into troubled waters, and Khalil who, unlike his father, favored whatever government was in power, now motioned to the servants to begin serving. They came at once with large trays heaped with sweetmeats, salads, eggs, olives, *leben* in gold-rimmed glasses, cheeses, pickled eggplant and the flat, round *pitta*.

Moving from guest to guest, urging them to partake of the food, Khalil came to the two youths. He gave Fared a meaningful look which meant that his marriage had already been mentioned. Fared rose, took the special dishes which were set aside for his grandfather, and brought them to him.

As he approached, he heard old Yunis saying, "My grandson Abdul tells me that Fared is of a mind to marry. Is she of our sinew?"

Fared clenched his jaws; how he detested that viperous old man! Laila's father belonged to no *hamula,* and Yunis knew this very well. It was his way of hinting at a social inferiority.

"She is the daughter of Ibrahim Tabari, a man honorable in all his dealings, a man of inner worth," Abu Sa'id replied.

"But why seek outside our own when our own daughters are of an age to marry?" Yunis persisted.

Fared had difficulty restraining his laughter. Yunis had a flock of daughters without schooling, stupid hens, and so homely they should be wearing black *purdahs.*

"It is said that this daughter of Tabari is proud with learning and is to go off to the school in Jerusalem for even more learning," said the ancient who was seated next to Yunis.

"Also, it is said that she is forward and given to ways that are not suitable to a true daughter of our faith," offered another.

The guests drew their chairs closer to the elders sitting around the Old Warrior: The talk was now spiced with pepper. They knew that Yunis and some others were saddled with aging daughters, and for a youth to marry outside and beneath their *hamula* was desertion, almost a betrayal.

Now Shahadi spoke up, and Fared felt he would forever be in his debt. He said, "The girl is a true Moslem. She is wise, but modest. She is beautiful, but not vain. Fared is fortunate if Tabari accepts the proposal."

Abu Sa'id brought an end to this discussion by asking Yunis how his crops were faring, now that he had piped water into his fields. The talk turned to crops, of the rise in taxes, and this led to the inevitable question: Would there be war? All faces turned to Abu Sa'id, who spoke out firmly.

"It is expressly written in our Koran: 'Perhaps one day God shall visit peace upon you and your adversaries and create friendship between you.' He is mighty, gentle and merciful, so there is hope there will be peace."

Presently he nodded to Fared, who helped him to his feet. The old man blessed his kinsmen and left.

It was late afternoon when Laila saw Fared walking down toward the main street, and she slipped out of her house to meet him at the Tomb of the Holy Man. She reached the tomb before Fared did.

Laila heard the crunch of footsteps and knew, by the droop of his shoulders and the stormy look on his face, that Fared was the bearer of bad news. She put her hands caressingly around his face and said, "Nothing, but nothing, that has happened at the *hamula* can be as sad as the look on your face."

He put his arm slackly around her shoulder. They stood leaning against the low wall of the tomb, and were silent. When he finally began to speak, the words rushed out in such an angry torrent that, at first, she failed to understand him.

"They ought not to be so powerful . . . they control everything . . . he won't let the *fellaheen*, on either side of his land, use his piped water unless they pay him scandalous prices."

"Who, Fared, who?"

"Yunis. And in the village council only their word counts, and they said . . ." He stopped himself from telling her that one of them said that if there is war, and the Arabs win, they will kill all those who worked with the Jews, and the Tabaris would be the first to be shot. And to mask his agitation he bent down, slipped off a sandal and shook out a few pebbles.

He was speaking against the *hamula* and its power, and this was good, Laila thought, but he was saying nothing that mattered most about themselves. Several weeks ago, at the *kibbutz* campfire, he said that if the *hamula* spoke against their marriage, then it was up to him to decide what to do. He said nothing of that now. Why was he silent about what actually was said at the *hamula?*

And because she could no longer endure the suspense, she asked, "Fared, what did they say about us?"

"What they said does not matter. At home my grandfather said that I am not ready for marriage."

Very quietly she asked, "And you, what do you think?"

"I know I am ready," he said. "It is a matter for us alone to decide. I haven't taken my studies seriously, so I'll probably be rejected by the university or the one in Tel Aviv or the Technion. I must consider seriously what to do. But more than anything else, I want to marry you—as soon as we can."

"That is what I wanted to hear," she said, and then, with a teasing smile, she added, "And you don't have to bring my father the bride-price."

"Now that's an inducement to marry you," Fared said, and kissed her.

10

Adam, the Reluctant Israeli

The storm clouds were piling over Israel, massive and threatening. On May 18, Nasser ordered the United Nations Emergency Force to evacuate its positions along the borders of the Gaza strip, as well as from Sinai and Sharm-el-Sheikh. Israeli ships were denied the right to pass through the Gulf of Aqaba, thus blockading her port of Elath.

Broadcast in Hebrew from Radio Cairo, this news was being piped into the dining hall when Ora and Emmi came in for breakfast. They sat down with Avram, Noah and Amitai. Usually the *kibbutzniks* listened to the mispronunciations and faulted Hebrew of the Egyptian announcer with amusement, but the thrust of encirclement was no longer a laughing matter.

"If it's really their first war move, let's pray that

they shoot with the same accuracy as their announcer speaks Hebrew," Noah said.

And while Avram and the others laughed at the
Hebrew words the announcer had used that contra-
dicted the meaning intended, Emmi looked distracted. The news was unnerving; Yoram was now in
the Negev facing the Egyptians.

At the other end of the table, Avram saw her
strained look, the uneaten food, and he sensed her
fear. He said, "Late yesterday, the students in the
upper grades of the secondary school volunteered to
work in the fields from sunrise to class time, but we
haven't heard from the nursery population."

Smiling weakly, Emmi said, "They are willing but
are still having diaper problems," at which laughter
broke out across the table.

Thinning out the clusters of the tiny green
apples wasn't really work, Aviva thought. She loved
heights, and on the top rung of the ladder she could
reach the highest branches, and feel herself soaring
skyward. At first, she and Laila had called out lines of
poetry to each other which later in the day, they
would need to know for their English class, but a
tractor in a nearby field made such a clatter that they
had to give up the effort to be heard.

Aviva felt rather sad about cutting out the
perfectly formed apples that crowded the branches
like peas in a pod, and denying them the fullness of
growth so that the others could have more space.

Adam worked below her. Now and then, she
dropped an apple on his head. She missed the mark
more often than not, but now it fell on his skull with

a plop. "It's the pull of gravity!" she said, grinning.

"That pull is straight down—yours was at an angle!" Adam said, but he didn't seem annoyed.

"I'd much rather do this than go to my first class," she said. "Euclid. Ugh!"

"Geometry is easy—once you get the axioms and definitions."

"I wish I had your brains in math," she said.

"Nothing wrong with your brains that a little more use wouldn't help," he said.

"Thanks for the compliment," and she kicked out at him. The ladder swayed and toppled over. He caught her as she fell, stumbled and dropped to the ground with her in his arms. He held her close for a moment, before she pulled away.

Without a glance at him, she climbed back on the ladder. Neither of them spoke again until they were called for breakfast.

Working in the banana field Fared thought it odd that here, in the *kibbutz*, he could tell time by the way his stomach growled with hunger while, at home, he rarely had an appetite. He was famished, and he wondered if he could endure the wait until breakfast. Who ever heard of working before breakfast!

From the distance, the long green fronds of the banana trees looked exotic, but there was nothing romantic about lopping off the excess bark with a heavy rake. The ground was messy and covered over with husk. Some of it slipped into his sandals and scratched his feet.

Moshe kept chopping away without pause and

with a swinging rhythm that made the work seem effortless. He was, Fared thought, as friendly as a homeless pup, but in their room he kept playing his harmonica until a withering look from Adam made him pocket it.

Adam enjoyed teasing him and the boy took it good-naturedly but sometimes, when he had his fill of it, Moshe cut him short with a stinging sarcasm, then took his harmonica and blew his feelings into it. Adam stomped out of the room in disgust. When the door banged shut, Moshe smiled sweetly, almost apologetically at Fared, opened his books and set to work.

Now Moshe put down his rake, wiped the sweat from his face with the sleeve of his T-shirt, and leaned both arms on the handle. Fared rested, too. "It will be a good crop, our first," Moshe offered. "We will ship them to Europe. There is even better soil for bananas below where the barns are. It was abandoned during the War of Independence. When the Yunis family returned from across the border, they got back some of the land, but the rest of it is a matter for the courts."

Fared, who had been listening only vaguely, now focused his attention at the mention of the Yunis family. Yunis. Abdul Yunis. His evil self.

Last Friday his father had excused him from attending services at the mosque because of a stomach upset. Actually, he had pretended a sickness to avoid seeing Abdul. It had been a mistake; he had proved to himself his own weakness. Why was he afraid to face Abdul? Nor had he gone to meet Laila at the Tomb of the Holy Man, and this was his

second mistake because Abdul, hearing of his indis-
position, came to the house.

They had stood on the terrace, talking of incon-
sequential things, and then they sauntered along the
path that sloped down to the village road. Abdul
seemed to be steering him toward it, but Fared
decided to go no farther. They would be passing in
full view of Laila's windows, and she would be hurt
that he had given up his usual time with her in favor
of Abdul.

Wittily Abdul told of some happenings in the
village when, without a pause and in the same light
vein, he asked, "Fared, when are you coming to a
meeting?"

Fared had been anticipating this question and
had rehearsed himself for just this confrontation, but
now he grew flustered at its suddenness. In his
confusion he stammered out, "How can I? All week
I'm up there and when I come home I—well—my
grandfather—I'm with him—mostly."

"You flew past our house last week in your car.
Was your grandfather with you?"

If it hadn't been for that smirk on Abdul's face,
Fared would have told him that racing his car was an
excitement he looked forward to all week. But there
was that contemptuous grin, and it stung him to the
quick. "It's none of your damn business what I do
when I come home!" He turned and started back to
his house when Abdul seized his arm. "You are a
weakling. We knew we could not count on you, and
the day will come when you will regret it!"

Moshe's voice broke in on his thoughts, "Fared,
are you all right?"

"Yes, why do you ask?" Fared snapped.

"You looked—well—like you were feeling sick. The breakfast call is late—here—have a fig."

Fared was no longer hungry and the fig smelled of things in Moshe's pocket, but he bit into it and it took away the bitter taste in his mouth.

After the noon meal that day, as Laila and Aviva were leaving the dining hall, Emmi came hurrying toward them. It was a warm day, and her face was flushed with the exertion of running from the children's area to the distant office building and then to the center where the dining hall was located. Her braided coronet hung slightly askew over her forehead. Seeing the two, she drew a deep sigh of relief.

"Aviva, the kindergarten teacher took sick. Ora said to draft you and Laila. We are to have our shelter practice."

Aviva frowned; she would miss biology—and she could not afford to miss it. Laila's face came alight. "Oh, I'd love it! Thank you for asking me—but I've no experience."

"It is really very simple," Emmi assured her. "I will explain everything. The children are nearly through with lunch, and they'll take their naps in the shelter. They're not at all difficult to manage; they're really little angels."

The nine children greeted Aviva with squeals of delight. When she introduced Laila, they speculated a moment before saying *"shalom,"* and then clamored for Aviva's attention. She told them to gather their books and toys, and it surprised Laila how effectively she managed them, without raising her voice.

The children were lined up and walked to the shelter. A cement stairway led down to a metal door.

Aviva switched on a light, and they came into the first of two long, narrow, whitewashed rooms. The ceiling was low but slightly arched, and this gave an effect of spaciousness. There were three tiers of bunks made of steel and attached by a chain to a post. Each bunk contained a mattress, covered over with a sheet, and a pillow. On the walls between the tiers hung the children's crayon drawings. Two chemical latrines stood between the two rooms.

On the wall opposite the bunks was the kitchen area with a refrigerator, an electric stove and a long, narrow table for dining as well as for the children's creative work. Small benches stood under it.

Laila, for whom the possibility of war had been too remote to give it more than a passing thought, now felt stunned as if she were experiencing the beginning of a terrible reality. She shuddered and, because Aviva was looking worriedly at her, forced a smile to her face and asked, "When will the rest come?"

"The kindergarteners? They're in isolation— they've been exposed to the measles," Aviva replied.

The children scrambled onto the bunks, and arguments broke out as to the possession of the top ones. Aviva settled it according to size; the smaller children had to be content with the lowest ones.

It was nap time and, while the children protested that they had not sufficiently inspected the premises, Aviva began helping the youngest ones undress and then, without further ado, dumped them onto their bunks.

"Five minutes for talk—then silence. Sleep!" she announced.

"But neither you nor I have a watch!" Laila whispered.

"True, but they don't know it."

The boy on the top tier hung over it with his chin propped on his fists, his large mournful eyes in his sallow face following Aviva as she picked up toys and books. "My daddy is in the army," he said matter-of-factly.

A rumpled towhead popped out from the bunk under him and called out, "My daddy is in the army, too!"

Rina, an active and mischievous little girl, was not impressed. "My daddy has a great big gun! It is so big it stands on three iron legs!"

"I know," Aviva said. "You all have very good daddies, very brave. Now quiet, everyone. Lie down, close your eyes, sleep!"

There were mutterings of protest but, within a few minutes, the noise subsided. Aviva beckoned Laila to the second room. When they reached it, a screech sent them flying back to Rina's bunk. She was sitting up with the wild stare of panic in her eyes.

"What is it, Rinaleh?" Aviva asked, smoothing back the web of black curls from her hot, tear-streaked cheeks.

"The Arabs! They will come and kill us!"

"Such nonsense! Your daddy won't let them! And all the other daddies! Remember the great big gun on the three iron legs?"

Rina thought on it, and began to feel safer, when her face screwed up tearfully again. "But why do they hate us?"

"Laila is an Arab and she doesn't hate us, do you, Laila?"

"Of course not!" Laila reassured her, and leaning down, she kissed the child.

"But if you like us, why don't you tell the other Arabs to be friends with us?" Rina asked.

"Well, it is rather difficult to explain it to a child," Laila said, and looked helplessly at Aviva.

Promptly Aviva took over. "Rina, last week, when I came to your room, you were pulling Yona's hair. Why?"

"Because he was pulling *my* hair!"

"Why?" Aviva insisted.

"Because he doesn't take care of his toys, and he always grabs mine because I take care so they are pretty always."

"Did you make up?"

Rina nodded.

"Well, that is how it is with the Arabs. They want our nice houses and our green fields, but your daddy with the great big gun and Yona's daddy and Shoshana's won't let them. And that will make the Arabs go back to their homes, and there will be *shalom* and we will all be friends. Now do you understand?"

Rina thought on this, and a new idea seized her and her black eyes danced. "If I gave the Arabs the presents I will get next month when I am five, will they stop being angry at us? I will tell everybody to send them presents, and it will be *shalom* for ever and ever, yes?"

"Yes, and now go to sleep."

Leaving the door ajar, the girls went out of the shelter and sat down on the steps. Emmi's piano tinkling came faintly across to them from the nursery, and over it they heard the high-pitched singing of the nursery children.

"It is terrible that they should know about hate, about war," Laila said, in a half-whisper.

"We can't shield them from a fact of life here. They must learn early the reality of things and live with them, or they'd grow up neurotics."

Laila was silent a moment. "It is so wasteful and immoral—this hate—so self-destructive. In our Koran it is written: 'Do not allow your hatred for other men to turn you away from justice. Deal justly. Justice is nearer to true piety.' "

"Our prophets said the same thing," Aviva said.

"That is what is so difficult to understand," Laila said. "Your people and mine are Semites. We should be closer, friendlier to each other than to any other people. We are, like your people, descendants of Abraham. Mohamet revered him, and Isaac, Jacob and Joseph. This is in our Koran. We have many of your customs—no pork meats—our boys are circumcised, too, and when they are thirteen are accepted into the faith."

There was a stirring in the shelter, a whispering, and the girls stood up. Just then a long pair of legs in blue jeans appeared on the top step, a lanky body bent down and Adam, a package under his arm, called down, "Aviva!"

"Be quiet! You will rouse the children!"

He tiptoed down a few steps and said, "I've a package—from Poland—let's have a *kumsitz* later. You come, too, Laila."

"Okay! Who else will be there?" Aviva asked.

"Fared, Adnan, maybe Erni."

"And Moshe?"

"That snot? He's only a kid."

"He is only eight months younger than you! Don't be so superior! What if there are only things to wear in the package?"

Adam held the box to his ears and shook it. He grinned. "Tins. Cookies and sweets."

"We'll be there," she said. "Be sure you ask Moshe. He's your roommate, so you'd better put a good face on and ask."

As he vaulted up the steps, Aviva said, "Now that's a switch! He always threw his mother's packages into the trash bin. I'll tell Erni, he'll be pleased. This morning, when we were pruning, Adam nearly kissed me."

"Yes, I saw," Laila smiled.

"Maybe he's becoming human. I used to feel sorry for him." She stopped at the first scream. "My God, the little angels are killing each other." The two ran into the shelter.

11

War Clouds Darken

In the waiting room of the *kibbutz* infirmary, Adam thought that if the woman who had just entered was called to Erni's office before him, he would leave. It would be an omen that what he had come to ask him to do would be refused.

At the telephone Malka was rattling off a list of supplies to someone. A door in the hall opened and a man emerged with Erni, who was giving him some instructions. In his white jacket he looked quite professional, Adam thought, almost as professional as a Polish doctor.

"*Shalom,* Adam," Erni called out from the open door. "Anything bothering you that can't wait a bit?"

"No—no," Adam said hesitantly as he unfolded himself to rise. "I—I have something to ask."

"Well then, if it isn't urgent, I'll see Chava first,"

he said and beckoned to the woman who had just entered.

Would Erni refuse his request? Or, granting it, would his father come after the many rebuffs he had given him? Nervously, Adam cracked his knuckles. His common sense should tell him that when your father comes the long distance from Jerusalem to see you on the *Shabbat* and you deliberately take off to avoid him, when you refuse to answer his phone calls or his letters, you have read yourself out of his life. That was how Adam had wanted it, and now, after several months of this treatment, his father had finally got the message.

What sort of person was this stranger, his father?

Was it true that he had conspired to wreck Poland's economy through "deceitful miscalculations" while he was an official on the Central Planning Commission? Would his wife have testified against him at his trial if he was innocent? And if he was innocent why, after his release from prison, had he not remained in Poland to vindicate himself?

Adam could not pinpoint the time when his real life suddenly ended, but he thought it was near his sixteenth birthday. He came home from a soccer game to find a man of cadaverous appearance, with a shaved, melon-shaped head, sunken eyes and grayish, collapsed cheeks that looked as if they had been sucked into the bones. His mother said, "Adam, this is your father."

It was not possible. He remembered his father as a tall and powerfully built man, with an air as if he were in command of an army, whose laugh was the merry roar of a giant. This was not even the shadow of that man, but a scarecrow smelling strongly of disinfectant.

From that moment on, he began to live on a split and descending level of existence. His father appeared before the Economic Planning Commission for reinstatement. The newspapers exhumed all the old charges against him, pointing up that the former convict was a Jew. All this reached into the class-room, and Adam's teacher seemed to have developed instant myopia—he could not see Adam's hand raised in answer to a question.

One day he was one of the six "inseparables" in his class, and the next day the inseparables looked through him as if he were invisible. He ceased being a Pole among Poles but was the Jew son of a Jew enemy of the State.

He felt that he had no place in the world.

There was no one with whom he could discuss all this and, when at last he spoke of this to his mother, she said, "Consider this from their position —wouldn't you do the same? A Communist boy does not honor the father who betrayed his country."

So he hated his mother with as much venom as he hated his father, and he even resented it because it interfered with this hate when that very same night she came into his room and sat beside him while he pretended to be asleep. But he knew she was weeping because, when she left, the pillow was wet.

At the end of the year, his father and he set out for Israel, and then they . . .

"Adam, come in," Erni called from his office.

"Have a good *kumsitz* the other night?" he inquired when Adam came in and sat down at the side of his desk.

"Not bad. Aviva brought over the electric kettle, and we had the cookies and candies she sent. She also sent a roll of film and asked that I send a picture of myself."

"Who is 'she'? "

"My mother. She likes me from a distance, so she bribes me to stay here with cookies and things."

"It could be she feels herself your mother."

"Strictly an illusion. Let's speak of another illusion—my father. I'd like you to phone him to come this *Shabbat* and bring a two-reed harmonica."

"Why don't you make the call?"

"He is finished with me. He hasn't written or phoned in over two months."

"Your father has been in touch with me regularly."

"He has?" Adam said and his voice rose in surprise. "But why, when I behaved the way I did."

"Let's say, he is still in search of his son. Do you want him to come so that he can bring the harmonica—or do you want him to come and bring it? And why a harmonica?"

Adam began pecking at his knuckles. "Because I threw Moshe's out the window. A truck ran over it."

Erni gave a low whistle. This seventeen-year-old was more sophisticated than any of his peers in the *kibbutz*—and yet so immature. He asked, "It wasn't your fault that the truck ran over it, so why get him a new one?"

Now Adam flushed, but his eyes held to Erni's. "That harmonica meant something to him. He is sort of lost without it. I know that feeling."

"Phone your father," Erni said. "But wait a few days. Last time we spoke, he was on army maneuvers."

"My father? But he's an old man!"

"The army doesn't think so. Didn't you know he is an officer in the Israeli reserves?" Adam said and shook his head. "Some day you ought to let yourself know your father—it will make you proud."

The phone at his elbow rang. His voice was terse when he spoke into it, "Dr. Mahler here. Now? *Tov!*"

Rising, he said, "Walk me to the office. As I was about to tell you—write him a letter. It would be nice for him to find it when he returns."

The conference to which Erni was summoned was called because an Israeli army officer had come to discuss *kibbutz* defense preparations. Seated at a large table were Ora, Avram, Noah and several other *kibbutzniks,* among them Amitai, who, as usual, wore his cowboy hat.

The officer was a medium-sized wiry man in his late twenties, with skin as dark as mahogany, a thin, humped nose and black eyes that were piercing and lively. His name was Mordecai, a captain in the Northern Command of the Department of the Military, in charge of Syrian and Lebanese borders. Yemen-born, he had served with Erni in the same army unit in the Sinai War, and had made the military his career.

"Erni!" he cried elatedly and, bouncing out of

his chair, he gripped the other's hand. "How was America?"

"One long ball, as the Americans say."

"Once, the Law came out of Zion and now our boys leave it to study."

"I didn't study law, you donkey."

"Same difference. We've got our own universities here—the best!"

Avram grinned as he watched them greet each other with warm camaraderie, and resumed the discussion interrupted by the greeting. "Erni, we were telling Mordecai what we need in the way of defense."

"We are short of everything but guts," Erni said.

"We've Uzis, submachine guns, but not enough for resistance if the Syrians break through. We need the heavy hardware," Avram said.

Mordecai looked up from his note-taking. "How about the fortification on top of the grazing field?"

"A few days ago we poured cement for the gun emplacements," Avram replied. "We haven't been wasting time—we've built shelters and zigzag trenches. We have worked out a detailed plan for the division of work and defense. Here is a copy." He sent a few typed sheets sailing across the table to the officer.

After glancing at them, Mordecai rose and studied the map of the *kibbutz* on the wall. "You haven't provided for connecting trenches between the buildings to the shelters."

"We've already detailed men to begin the work," Ora put in.

"Let's have a look around," Mordecai said, but

made no move to rise. His lean body remained relaxed in the chair as he looked with a questioning smile at the grave faces around him.

"Mordecai, when will it start?" Ora asked.

"Soon, we think," he replied. "If it comes, the Air Force will be concentrated in the south, because of heavy Egyptian concentration in the Sinai, so you will have to take the brunt of the fighting here."

"President Johnson—the English—the French—keep urging us to restrain ourselves, but who is restraining Nasser?" Noah asked querulously. "Tiran is still blockaded. We need a new Moses to open the sea!"

And Amitai, who had participated only by listening, now broke his silence. "Here we also need a new head," he said and looked dourly at Ora. "We are worried about the enemy at the borders, but what about the enemy among us?"

Mordecai shot upright in his chair like a sprung arrow. "What do you mean?"

"Ask Ora. She knows what I mean."

Ora told the officer about the work-study group. He tugged at his ear and remarked, "A ticklish situation."

"They're a good bunch—loyal Israelis," Avram assured him. "Their parents are our friends from many years back."

"It takes only one of them to lay a mine, to make a map of our fortifications, to pinpoint gun emplacements," Amitai hinted.

"When does school close here?" Mordecai asked.

"In about a month," Ora replied.

"It's a problem we'll have to consider, but right

now let's take a look at the strategic places," Mordecai said as he rose.

Moving to the door with Erni, the officer gave him a resounding clap on his shoulder. "Tell me some good news. How many babies were born here this year?"

"Three so far. Several more are due."

"Only three?" Mordecai's brows raised in surprise.

"Living under those Syrian guns is not exactly an inducement to a higher birth rate," Erni replied.

"Are you married?" Mordecai asked and then added, when Erni shook his head, "We're both the same age—and already I have four children!"

"The girl I want still has some growing up to do," Erni said, to which the officer retorted, "That's when to marry her—before her mind matures. Believe me—this I know!"

"You probably do. Four children!" Erni gave a low whistle as he followed him to his jeep.

Later that day, in the same room, Avram and Erni were looking at several snapshots while Ora, her face stony with anger, waited for their comments.

"Not bad, but I wouldn't recommend Fared as a photographer," Avram commented.

"He does not know how to use light and shade," Erni observed.

"Suppose you look at them more closely," Ora said with an edge of sarcasm.

"What's so challenging about these pictures?" Erni asked. "Adam looks self-satisfied, sort of lord of the roost with his arms around Aviva and Laila.

His mother should be pleased at how well he looks."

"And that's all you see—Adam and the girls? How about the pictures of just Adam?" Ora asked. And then, as they scrutinized the pictures, she saw a frown deepening on Avram's face, and she said, "That's right. Each picture of Adam alone is against a background of a strategic defense position."

"Good God—yes!" Erni exclaimed.

"Who has the negatives?" Avram asked.

"I have," Ora replied. "Adam wanted two sets, and Moshe ran out of paper. He gave them to me. Let's speak to Fared, and I wish to God Adam would decide to return to Poland!"

"Aren't you premature—rushing to judgment?" Erni said.

"I'll get Fared—he's with the others waiting to be taken home for their *Shabbat*," Ora said and hurried out.

"Ora usually looks on the negative side of things," Avram said gloomily.

"Could be you're right," Erni agreed without conviction.

When Fared came into the room, he gave the two men a friendly wave of the wrist. When Ora handed him the pictures, he looked pleasantly surprised. "Moshe is a good developer. I took them."

"Why did you choose those particular places?" Ora asked.

"We just kept climbing until we saw what would be good views," Fared replied. Then, seeing how grave they were, he asked, "Is there anything wrong?"

"What else besides the view did you aim for?" Avram asked.

"The rusty artillery on the old military field above the grazing field—we picked flowers there several weeks ago," Fared answered unself-consciously, frowning in puzzlement at the questions. All at once it dawned on him what other unspoken thought Avram meant by his question, and the blood drained from his face. Last month Abdul had asked about the position of gun emplacements, but he had dismissed it so completely from his mind that actually all he had seen on the high field was the disused gun, the newly laid cement bed and the Syrian hills towering over it.

He felt as if his bones were dissolving, and he dropped heavily into a chair. Then, as the silence lengthened and all eyes focused on him, his face took on a frightened and bewildered look. "I—I had nothing else on my mind but taking the picture that Adam wanted to send his mother!"

Wetting his lips, he cried out in a hoarse voice, "In Allah's name, I am telling you the truth, and you must believe me!"

"I do believe you," Erni said promptly.

Ora saw the torment in the face. It was not the look of one trapped in guilt, but the shock of an innocence that is rejected. She let out her long-held breath and said quietly, "Yes, Fared, I believe you. Let's go."

Why did Erni have the snapshots? Adam wondered. At first, the question puzzled him and then worried him when he saw Fared coming out of the office with Ora. Fared looked ghastly, and his eyes slid away from Adam's guiltily. What was it all about? He would have spoken to Fared, but he leaped onto the back of the truck to return to his home.

"Ora said you have my pictures," Adam said when he came into Erni's office. He felt that Erni's greeting was less than cordial.

Picking up the snapshots on his desk, Erni handed them to him. Adam glanced at them and lingered over a picture of himself and Aviva outside their school.

Erni filled his pipe and tamped it thoughtfully. "Sit down, Adam."

His tone was quite casual, but Adam sensed something, some kind of strain. He watched Erni separating the pictures into two sets, those of him with the girls at the *kibbutz* buildings, and those of him alone on the higher levels.

"Adam, why did you choose these backgrounds?"

"Are they off limits to me? No one said anything."

"No, they are not off limits to you, but we took it for granted that you would not pinpoint gun emplacements."

"What do you mean?"

"You asked Moshe for two sets—one for yourself and another for Fared. We trust both of you, but Fared—with the best intentions toward us—might show them to someone in his village who isn't so well intentioned."

"Aren't you being too suspicious?"

"Adam, we cannot afford not to be," Erni said crisply.

Adam picked up the two sets, tore them in half and threw the pieces on the desk. Then, scornfully, he said, "There, does that make you feel safer?"

"Adam, sit down!" Erni ordered.

Sullenly Adam sat down again, aware that this was no longer the friendly Erni with whom he found it possible to unburden himself. Erni was now the establishment, impersonal and critical.

"You confuse me, Adam. Just as I thought we were beginning to lick your problem, we're back where we were in the beginning. You are still making a conscious effort to hate everything and everybody here."

"That's not true! I like Aviva. . . ."

"You would like the others, too, if you let yourself."

"And I don't mind you."

"Did you ever feel yourself a Jew in Poland?" Erni now asked.

"We were all Poles!" Adam said haughtily.

"We were all Germans—until the Germans refused to let us remain Germans!"

"We observed the anniversary of the Warsaw Ghetto—and the victims of the holocaust. . . ."

"Adam, what is a holocaust?"

"What the Germans did."

"No! I refuse to label the murder of six million Jews a holocaust! A holocaust is a natural force—like an earthquake or a cyclone—and cannot be averted by man. This was not a natural phenomenon; it was the Germans who let loose all the elements of destruction. And that is what is happening in Poland —in Russia—it began as anti-Semitism, and it led to extermination camps!"

When he fell silent, he picked up his pipe again, emptied the ashes, and filled it with a sweet-smelling tobacco from a tin on his desk. His tone, when he spoke again, no longer had the biting hardness that had stunned Adam.

"You are still unhappy here, Adam, aren't you? If you wish, we can arrange to send you back to Poland."

"Does my father want me returned?"

"We discussed it. He said to give you time. You are here a full year now."

"Do you want me to leave?"

"It has to do with what you want. At times your behavior makes me think you and Poland deserve each other."

Adam's smile was sheepish. "My behavior is rather infantile," he said.

"Indeed, it is."

"And if I decide to remain?"

"You'll have to stop pitying yourself as a bleeding Polish patriot in exile and think of yourself as an Israeli. You'll have to get with it, as the Americans say. Ask yourself some very basic questions—soon. Time is a commodity we're rather short of, and planes leaving for Europe will soon be in short supply, too."

Without smiling, he dismissed Adam with a nod. He did not look up when Adam rose but, opening a folder on his desk, began reading.

12

The Terrorists Strike

Reading the slips of paper, spiked on the branches of the tree that arched over the Tomb of the Holy Man, Laila marveled at the naive and enduring faith of the women of her village. Her neighbor, Latifa, whose prayers last month had been for a son instead of a fifth daughter, was now nursing her fifth daughter, and yet here, on the lowest limb of the tree, was another petition from her pleading for the return to health of her husband Tewfik, who was in the hospital.

Faith was essential to hope, Laila thought, but faith that resigned itself to utter passivity was self-deluding. Laila believed devoutly in prayer, but she acted toward its fulfillment, and was convinced that all her prayers to pass the entrance examinations at Hebrew University would not be answered if she did not work at her studies.

The other day Ora had asked her what she would do with her education and she replied, "I keep wavering between being a scientist, a teacher or a psychologist. Shouldn't I know by now what I want to be? It worries me, this indecision."

"Don't worry. At the university, it will come to you."

And now, suddenly, it came. She wanted to help the village women to reach into books, and learn and discover their particular selves as she had, and to come to an awareness that they count for something as human beings.

A thrill went through her as she envisioned herself in this role, and then it struck her how little she really knew, how much she had yet to learn . . . had she the capacity to?

"Leave some grass for the goats!"

Fared stood grinning down at her. She had not even heard his footsteps, while she sat mindlessly tearing the grass, wrinkling her new print dress.

"But better the grass than my hair. Am I very late?" he asked with his disarming smile, as he sat down beside her. "A new dress! Very pretty—the cornflowers deepen the blue of your eyes. Am I very late?"

"I don't know, you have a watch. How is Abu Sa'id?"

"Miraculous how he keeps improving. My father thinks it is because of our prayers, and I think my grandfather's iron will, plus Erni's injection, keeps him alive. Laila, don't go back to the *kibbutz* to-night!"

"But Aviva invited me for the Sabbath dinner

and to help with the children at the swimming pool tomorrow."

"Leave it for the next time," he said urgingly.

"With things as they are, who can be sure of a next time. But why don't you want me to go?"

"Because my father is coming to your house tonight. He will discuss—our marriage." He said this quietly, but his eyes glittered with a contained excitement.

"But you were so pessimistic after the *hamula* met . . . does that mean that Abu Sa'id approves of me?"

"It wasn't you—it was me he found lacking— and irresponsible. But he thinks better of me since I'm at the *kibbutz*—and I broke with Abdul."

"You did! Over what?"

"Well, we stopped agreeing—on—on things. But I haven't told you the rest of it. My grandfather thinks I should have a tutor and bone up for the exams. He mentioned the son of Shahadi who teaches at the government school here and who graduated from Hebrew University. What's wrong, Laila?"

She had dropped her face into her hands. Her eyes brimmed with tears when she lifted them to Fared. "It all sounds too good to be true. I'm frightened—it's just too wonderful."

"Everything depends on—well—if I can keep my mind on my studies. I'm not a student like you."

"But with a tutor and me to help—of course you'll pass! You've never even tapped your potential and it's there!"

Fared hugged her. They were silent a while, and then he said moodily, "You're the only one who has real confidence in me. I'm selfish and light-minded and unsettled, but of one thing I am certain—you are the best thing that's happened in my life, and I will sweat over those books—I promise. And you will not regret that you married me."

She burrowed her head deeper into his arms.

Later, as her father drove her to the *kibbutz,* she felt she would burst with all the excitement locked inside her. But how could she tell him without revealing that she had secretly met Fared? She began to chatter about things in the village, small bits of gossip the women had told her that morning, while the men were in the mosque. Once, she caught a quizzical smile on his face, and she surmised his thoughts. She was not an idle chatterer and he must sense that underneath the mindless flow of words was something serious and unspoken.

"I'll drop in on Noah," he said as he slowed to a stop before the *kibbutz* buildings. He kissed her forehead. Suddenly she felt shaken by some unknown fear and threw her arms around him. He touched her cheek with the tips of his fingers, his habitual gesture now that she was a grown girl, and his eyes held such love that she felt comforted. She smiled and quickly walked away, feeling excitement at sharing her wonderful news with Aviva, and regretting that she would not be home that evening when those things would be discussed that would forever change her life.

Coming to the first lane of cottages, she saw that the flower beds were yielding to trenches, sandbags were being placed around the walls of cottages and windows were already crisscrossed with tape. Overnight, the *kibbutz* had taken on a grim look. She had seen the social buildings protected this way, but not the dwellings, and she went icy at the thought that soon, perhaps that very night, the Syrians would open fire.

When she came into her cottage, Moshe was helping Aviva tape a window. He gaped when he saw her, while Aviva exclaimed, "Such a pretty dress, Laila! *Shalom!*"

"She looks like a walking field." Moshe sputtered and stopped when the girls squealed with laughter. "I mean, so many cornflowers, they're so alive!"

"My mother made it at the Dress Coop," Laila said. "Aviva, yours is very pretty, too." She wished that Moshe would finish and leave, so that she could confide her news to Aviva. Now the windows were taped, but he dropped into a chair and reached for the plate of cookies.

"We're going for a walk, Moshe," Aviva announced.

"I'll go along," he said and jumped to his feet.

The girls exchanged commiserating glances which he caught. "You needn't shout—I got the message!" and he stalked out the room. Aviva flew after him.

"Moshele, don't be angry," she said coaxingly as she smoothed back his rumpled hair. "Laila and I have things to talk over. Save us seats at the table tonight."

When he was finally out of sight, Laila asked, "How did you know I had something to tell you?"

"Your eyes—they were popping with excitement."

Aviva hugged her wildly when Laila told her the news. "You are my first friend to marry! And I've never been to an Arab wedding. Ora has, and some of the others. When, Laila?"

"They'll discuss it tonight," she said and began to explain Arab marriage customs. In the midst of it, the two girls burst into tears and comforted each other with vows of enduring friendship.

Then, arms linked, they left the house.

They walked along the winding lanes of dwellings and exchanged Sabbath greetings with people strolling past them, and with those sitting on verandas, relaxing in the pleasant late afternoon sunshine.

Children romped about on the lawns, playing with their parents. A little girl, with a red bow on her dark curls, screamed, "Catch me *Abba*," and ran across the lawn to the road, then screamed again in a higher key when she tumbled over. Aviva bent down and tried to stand her upright. "Get up Rina! You're not hurt!"

"Go away. I want my daddy!"

A heavy-set young soldier came running, the ends of his khaki shirt flapping at the sides. He swung the child onto his shoulder and said, "*Shalom*, Vivi, I get more exercise here in one day than at the post all week."

"Be of good courage, Dudi, you've still got all of tomorrow with Rina," Aviva said laughingly.

The girls resumed their walk and turned into the hill road. "Are we going up all the way?" Laila asked.

"No, just a short climb. It's where we were supposed to build our swimming pool."

The sky was becoming a starry sapphire and a bluish dusk was enveloping the field. As they walked, Aviva said, "I used to think when I was younger that people are free spirits and shouldn't be pinned down to one person."

"Not even if you fall in love?" Laila asked.

"That's when I stopped being a free spirit and wanted to be pinned down," Aviva admitted with a little laugh. "He was not in Israel at the time, and I would torment myself thinking that he would marry."

"And now that Erni is back?"

Startled, Aviva exclaimed, "But how did you know?"

"You don't act like yourself when he is with us."

"Oh, how observant you are! I feel so shallow compared to him that I behave like a childish brat. Maybe that's because he never stops treating me as if he was my elderly uncle."

"Recognizing your problem is half its solution," Laila assured her.

There was a pine scent in the air, although the pines were on a higher field. They could see their spires as they came out to the hill road and then turned toward the dwellings.

Even though black paper had been pasted to the window frames of the dining hall for the night blackout and the pictures had been removed from the walls, Laila thought that the large room had a very festive look. The tables were covered with white cloths, with candles and flowers making a cheerful glow of brightness and color.

Moshe stood up and waved to them. He began to tell them something when Aviva silenced him with a warning finger to her lips; men were rising to make the *kiddush* and they remained standing as Noah intoned the ancient prayer.

The food was delicious and of such abundance that Laila could not eat it all, and Moshe relished the rest. Then, as the meal progressed to dessert, the room became jolly with song. Noah struck up a lively *zmira,* which was a table hymn. One song followed another, and it was always Noah who led off.

As the singing went on Laila suddenly felt lonely. She wanted to be with Fared. She wanted to be home where decisions were now being made for her. Did her father think better of Fared now that he had revealed himself a more responsible person? Had his father really come?

She was torn out of her musing by Erni and swept into a *hora.* Tables had been pushed against the wall to make room for the dancing. And Emmi, at the piano, caused laughter and some confusion when, without a pause, she went from a *hora* to a polka, then a waltz and even ventured to American rock, and finally wound up with a Russian dance.

It was nearly midnight when Noah, who had been hopping around in some intricate and lively Russian steps, in the center of the ring, reeled forward, staggered and fell. Erni was bending over him before anyone was aware that this was no longer part of the dance. When Noah recovered, he said, "When an old fool forgets he is old, it is time to put him to bed."

"Exactly where you're going," Ora agreed and, holding one arm while Avram took a firm grip on the other, they took him home. The dancing ended.

"Do you think he is very ill?" Laila asked Aviva, as they walked back to their cottage in the eerie light cast by the hooded lamps.

"My grandfather is indestructible," Aviva said, with a defiant toss of her head as if challenging fate. Then, wistfully, she added, "It isn't like old times anymore. I miss Yoram—the others. We always had such jolly campfires on the *Shabbat.*"

"They will happen again," Laila said reassuringly.

"As Noah would say, 'From your mouth to God's ear.'"

They laughed but it was a hollow sound in the dark, and mirthless. Suddenly, they felt tired and, for some incomprehensible reason, quite sad.

On the Sabbath, breakfast was a leisurely enjoyment for the *kibbutzniks.* The discipline of the early meal was relaxed, and late-risers knew that the kitchen workers would not turn them away unfed. Some brought trays of food to the cottages, while parents headed for the children's section for a day of togetherness with them.

Accustomed to the early rising here, Laila woke at the usual time and to the thought that, one way or another, her fate had been decided last night. She felt a tremor of nerves. How could she survive the day without knowing, she had asked Aviva.

"Telephone your father, you goose!" Aviva advised.

"But we do not have a telephone. There is one in the machine Coop, but they're always out on jobs."

"Then keep trying until someone does answer."

"But we are going to the swimming pool!" Laila reminded her.

"Well, let's get started. We've got to get you a swim suit." Then, after they had showered and dressed, Aviva said, "Fared's people have a telephone. They ring here for Erni—and Ora telephones to find out how Abu Sa'id is. Why don't you call?"

Shocked, at the proposal, Laila said, "But that is not done—it would be almost as bold as—well—as proposing!"

"What's wrong with that? I proposed two years ago to Erni before he left for New York!"

"What did he say?"

"He touched the back of my ears and said, 'Not dry enough, girl, you've still some aging to do,' " and they broke into laughter.

The children were still at breakfast and the girls climbed onto the rear of the truck which had benches on both sides nailed down its length.

"Ugh! They didn't clean it yet!" Aviva cried, and with Laila helping, picked up odd pieces of clothing, scraps of paper, a plastic ball, some apple cores, and a few blue caps.

"Forbidden!"

The stern command startled Laila, and looking up saw Noah wagging an admonishing finger at her. His eyes twinkled with teasing. He looked so hearty, it seemed as if last night's collapse hadn't even happened.

"On the *Shabbat* we work only to feed the livestock, the two- and four-legged ones," he said.

Just then Ora appeared. She looked critically at him and scolded, "You were told to stay in bed all day!"

"On a golden day like this! A criminal waste!"

As she urged him back to bed, she kept scanning the earth at the sides of the road for the telltale change of color that would reveal if it had been tampered with. Yesterday Avram had uncovered and defuzed a mine at the machine building.

"Laila, there was a phone call for you," Ora said. "We looked for you in your room and in the dining hall."

"Who was it?" Laila asked, in a whispery voice, as her heart thumped wildly.

"Fared. He left a message. He said he now considers himself your father's fourth son. Does that make sense to you?"

Laila's hands flew to her face and, when they came away, her eyes glittered with tears. "Yes, oh yes! Of course it does!"

"Does it!" Aviva screamed excitedly. "It only means that Ibrahim agreed to let her marry Fared!"

"A wedding! *Mazel Tov,* Laila!" Noah cried.

"Laila, would you like me to drive you home now?"

Laila's face lit up and instantly clouded. She had felt proud and elated when they had asked her to help with the children—and now she felt torn between the urge to go home and the obligation to her given word. She said, "We are to return around noon. Will you take me then?"

"Of course!" Ora promised.

"Let's speed the little angels along," Aviva said when Ora walked away.

A sudden flash of light—a hot thrust of wind snapped her head back and, even before she heard the blast, Ora stood rooted to the spot, while a sickening wave of pure terror went through her. Screams broke out. She ran back to the truck.

She reached Noah first. He lay in the relaxed posture of sleep. Near him, face down, Aviva was screaming with all her strength as she clawed the earth. All at once there was a crowd. Erni came running.

"Vivi, don't be frightened. Erni is coming," Ora said and crawled around the pool of blood between the girls to Laila. Glassy with terror as Ora bent over her, Laila's eyes now focused on Ora with an imploring look. Blood gushed out of a gaping hole under her breast. Someone held out towels and, in an icy calm, Ora tore open the dress and began stanching the flow of blood. The slender young body gave a violent shudder and then lay still. Ora was only vaguely aware that Erni was on his knees beside Laila, until he said, "It's no use, Ora."

Ora gaped at him, too stunned to cry out. Then she gave a low moan, and he helped her to her feet. "Aviva? Noah?" she asked.

"A thigh wound. Noah?" he said and shrugged. "I'm not calling for an ambulance—it will take too long to get here. We'll take them in the truck."

Avram pushed through the crowd and Ora said

tonelessly, "Laila's dead. Phone the Coop—they'll get Ibrahim. Then take Laila home."

The knock on his door was louder now, and his father's voice more commanding. "Fared, come with us to Ibrahim!"

Dream-haunted, Fared buried his head deeper into the pillow. If he left his room, he would lose Laila. She had come into it with him immediately after the funeral, and she had occupied it like a living presence, as tangible to his touch as his own body, her voice more audible to him than those who spoke urgingly outside his door. If he let them in, it would shatter their oneness.

He could not go to the house of mourning.

He tried to rise. A cold sweat broke out over him and, trembling, he fell back. He was frightened. He did not know what it was that frightened him so. Suddenly he felt himself unable to breathe. He dragged himself to the window and drew in great gulps of air.

And then, all at once, it struck him and he said, "Laila is dead." And then, "She is dead because I kept silent."

It was out at last, the guilt to which he dared not give thought or words. If he had not kept silent, if he had told his grandfather, or even his father, Laila would be alive today. She had said, "Ours is a destructive nationalism," when the field in the *kibbutz* had been destroyed, and he had agreed with her, but how could he inform on Abdul? He, Fared, was as guilty of her death as the one who had planted the mine.

He was frightened by the enormity of his guilt and, suddenly, he was at the door and out the house.

As if drawn by a magnet, he came to the Tomb of the Holy Man and stopped. There, on the farther hill, was her grave with the bright red crowns of geraniums that Adam and Moshe had planted. He turned and strode away. He walked aimlessly.

Presently, he found himself at the low, fenced-in *kibbutz* wheatfield that lay adjacent to Yunis's land. Surveyors were setting up their equipment. One of them, whom he knew, nodded. An Israeli soldier called out, "What are you doing here?"

The friendly surveyor said that Fared was okay, the grandson of Abu Sa'id el Khoury. The soldier waved him on. Farther on, the earth was bare and cracked open, and was striated by a *wadi* that ran its zigzag course down from the demilitarized zone. Beyond it, bulging skyward, was the Syrian escarpment.

"Fared!"

The dreaded voice shook him and he stood transfixed, as Abdul strode toward him. Neither spoke when he came abreast but stood measuring each other. And then Fared rasped out, "You killed Laila. You laid the mine."

Abdul fixed his eyes on Fared with his steady, penetrating stare. Fared met it unflinchingly.

"Fared, don't say that again. For your own good, don't. There are too many like you who reconcile yourselves to being Israelis. In the war, we'll finish off the lot of you."

Rage exploded in Fared and he lunged at Abdul, knocking him down, pinning him flat to the ground with his knees. He saw Abdul's eyes bulge with terror and his grip round his neck tightened. A wild passion went through him. If he killed Abdul now it would be an act of retaliation, of redemption, and justifiable in Moslem law. Then, he would be free forever of his guilt to Laila.

He heard the soldier's shouts. His hold on Abdul loosened, and he released him. Fared could kill him without remorse for what he had done, but could not hand him over to the Israeli soldier. "Get up, you murderer!" he hissed.

Abdul struggled to his feet, wincing with pain as he clutched his arm. "You've broken it!"

They heard the rustling sound of movement through the dry rushes. The surveyors and the soldiers.

"Will you hand me over to them?" There was a jeering note in Abdul's voice and his eyes held a challenge.

Before Fared could reply, the men began setting up their equipment. The soldier stood nearby.

Without answering Abdul, Fared walked away.

13

An Old Pioneer Fades Away

Aviva felt no pain when the drug wore off, nor did she feel panic that the right side of her body, from the hip down, was encased in plaster. Yesterday, before her second operation, Erni explained everything to her—there was a good possibility that the leg would be saved. She said, "Better lame than dead," and he had kissed her.

The wailing of the two Arab women, from opposite sides of the room, made Aviva sleepy, and she wondered why the nurse had not put them alongside each other.

The monotonous drone of their voices lulled Aviva into a pleasant euphoria—a feeling as if she were swinging gently in space, deliciously content because she was free of pain. And then a sudden thought wrenched her to awareness. Laila! What had happened to Laila? In the past few days, pain and terror of what awaited her in the operating room had drawn her utterly into herself, but now it was unbearable not to know about Laila. And yet, instinctively, she knew.

She turned her head away from the glare of sunlight and gave a start when she saw Adnan on the chair near her, the field flowers he clenched drooping on his lap. He was staring into space, but his eyes held such deep sorrow that instantly she knew.

"It's true, Adnan, isn't it? Laila is dead." She touched his hand lightly and he gave a quick shudder, but then that tender smile came to his face.

Her eyes smarted, but no tears came. Then, because she felt a compelling need to recall it all, she said, "We were both crazy happy the minute—before. Fared had phoned, so that Laila knew. I did a cartwheel, and she tried to and flopped over, and we sat on the ground howling with laughter. Then we leaped up to race each other to the children's house and before we even started—it happened."

Adnan did not speak but tears welled up and he turned his head aside. He rose. Aviva knew his need to weep and knew that he would not do this in front of her.

"Aviva, do not think life is over if . . . if . . . ," and he gulped back the words. "That is how I felt when I lost my leg. But you danced with me—so you see—it is the same with both of us. Do not despair."

She smiled wryly. It was not the same.

"She loved you, Aviva," Adnan said softly, and he left.

She heard Ora greeting him in the hall, but it

was Avram who presently came into the room. At first, with his bouncy walk, his brush-short hair, his bronzed face and stocky build she thought it was Yoram. He kissed her cheek.

"Avram! It's the first kiss in years!"

"You're like a butterfly—there's no pinning you down long enough for one. You look fit enough to come home."

"And so she will—soon," Ora said as she came in.

"*Ima!* Where have you been all day?"

"Here. But you were asleep. I visited with Noah."

"How is he?"

"He keeps drinking what he says is warmed up gall, but the nurse insists it is tea."

Then, plaintively, Aviva said, "It's over for me, *Ima*."

"What is over?"

"My dancing."

"You are talking nonsense."

"But it is! I dreamed of living life to the fullest—and a career was my dream of living. . . ."

"It is only part of a way of life. To love is to live life to the fullest," Ora said.

"In this room, a patient isn't allowed more than one visitor at a time!" Erni announced from the door.

"I will drop in on Noah," Avram said and, beckoning Ora, left the room with her.

"Well, I guess this finishes my chances of going to ballet school," Aviva said, with a tap of her knuckles on the cast.

"Well, you definitely won't go today or tomorrow. In a few months, probably," Erni said.

"You know as well as I that it's over for me!"

"I'll get you a professional's shingle. Diagnostic pessimism is rather unusual for a freshman doctor, but then you're an unusual girl."

"It's not like you to flatter—and don't be sarcastic!" Then, with a heavy sigh, she added, "Oh well, I might have been only a mediocre dancer."

"Then you can always marry me. I'm a mediocre person. We'll pair off just fine."

"Erni, stop teasing! I'm in no mood for it. Go away. I want to think about things. No, stay, please!" And then, brokenly, she sobbed out, "I know about Laila."

In the corridor Ora asked Avram, "Did you pick them up?"

"None of them showed up at the collection point. I spoke to Ibrahim, and he said the parents are afraid to let them go. Just as well—our people are a bit nervous now."

"I know. Amitai's been talking—but only a few agree with him. They all feel heartsick over Laila," Ora said.

"How is Noah?"

"None of the doctors know what's keeping him alive. At times there is no pulse and only a feeble, erratic heartbeat."

Noah was sipping a pale, lemony liquid through a glass tube when they came in. He grimaced. "Ora, I don't want a stone on my grave. Put a *cheinik* on it instead, a real old-fashioned teakettle, not an electrical one. Where I'm going—maybe it's not modern with electricity. Avram, did they come?"

"No, they're still mourning Laila," Avram replied.

Noah reproached him with a look. "Stop telling me grandma tales. It's like the old days when the Arabs called us Children of Death and stayed away from us. Only Abu Sa'id came. . . ." His voice trailed away.

Children of Death. Ora smiled wryly at the long unheard name that the Arabs once called them. It summoned up the old pioneering days when building the *kibbutz* was a fever burning in their blood, to which was added the fever shoveled out of the pestilential swamps where, the Arabs said, lived the Evil Spirit and, for disturbing it, the Jews would surely die. And die they did. But after those many deaths and after the swamps were drained, there was no more malaria for Jew or Arab.

"Yes, war or not, Abu Sa'id will surely come," Noah's voice was hardly more than a sigh, and then a smile touched his lips and he added, "If only to see me buried."

It seemed to Ora that as the light dimmed inside Noah and the shadow of death seeped into his face, his lips still held the curve of a smile.

Every morning before the *kibbutzniks* went to work, army sappers came to check for mines. This was usually completed by the time the work day began. But on the morning that Aviva was brought home, just as the soldiers were putting their detectors on the truck, a sergeant looked warily at a saucer-shaped button on one of the dirt roads at the edge of an orchard. On closer inspection he uncovered wires, and farther along, between two trees, a mine. As it was defuzed, the mine exploded, but, miraculously, the sapper was not hurt.

The blast greeted Aviva, who sat in the cab of the truck between Ora and Erni.

"They're probably dynamiting a boulder up on the military field," Erni said, and wondered at the lie.

"No—a twenty-one gun salute for me!" Aviva said.

"That, too," Erni agreed.

"Oh, but it's marvelous to be home again!" Aviva cried as the truck chugged up the steep grade and onto the road of buildings. She reached over to the wheel and thwacked ecstatically on the horn, waving as first one startled face and then another came to the window.

"*Ima*, you've passed my lane!"

"You're to stay with me for a while," Ora said as she wheeled to a stop before the two-story house. She picked up the pair of crutches.

"But I want to use them!" Aviva insisted, when Erni lifted her down, and she struggled to be put on her feet.

"Stop fussing," he said, as he carried her into the house and laid her on the couch. "For the next few days you use them only to go to the bathroom. Later, we'll see, but you're to follow instructions precisely as you were told, or back to the hospital you go. Here we have no time for children with tantrums."

"Erni, if once, just once, you treated me as if I were an adult, rather than a retarded child, I'd behave maturely."

"Possibly. I'll try it some day. But for the next few weeks, you know what you should or shouldn't do!"

When he left Aviva said, "We always seem to annoy each other." Ora gave her a pill and a glass of water.

"Erni was very worried—he'd dash down to the hospital before six every morning, consult with the doctor, look in on you, fly back here and tend to the sick—then guard duty. You can't keep an even temper on four hours of sleep."

Aviva was silent a while, thinking, if I can get a balance between the child and the grown-up in me, I'd be all of a piece, like Laila. Aloud, she said, "*Ima,* what's been happening while I was away?"

With a clap of her hands, Ora said, "A big excitement! It happened last week when Amitai glanced out the window and said, 'We have guests!' And there they were—our friends from Umm Tubas, in trucks and a tractor. The *Mukhtar,* Ibrahim and his sons, others, Fared and the rest of the work-study group, and they all volunteered to work with us."

A pensive look came to her face, and she lapsed into silence. Three glorious days of working together . . . the dining hall alive with laughter. And then, on the evening of the third day, the Syrian broadcast: "Israel is doomed. All the Jews will be annihilated together with those Arabs who work for them." On the fourth morning, only Ibrahim, his three sons, and Fared came.

"Did Abu Sa'id come to Noah's funeral?"

Ora nodded. She could still see the grief carved on that noble old face. "Noah would have loved the speeches. Everyone remembered a particular thing he'd done for them—something wise or witty he'd said. Abu Sa'id did not speak—but the look on his face made you feel his grief. And Ibrahim spoke and the *Mukhtar* remembered a few good things the *kibbutz* did for Umm Tubas. I could almost hear Noah say, 'Enough talk already! Let's have the *cheinik!'* "

Aviva smiled tiredly. Ora placed the crutches within her reach on the floor. "Vivi, I have class now. Malka will stay until I return. Here are books but try to sleep."

"*Ima,* is Malka going to have a baby?"

"Yes, if she takes proper care. We've given her two weeks off from work. That is why she'll be free to stay here."

The door had hardly closed behind her when Aviva fell asleep. The room was in shadows when she awoke. There were flowers everywhere, some even festooned the African sculptures, and Ora was busy at the stove. There was a dish of cookies and a bowl of fruit on the table.

"It looks as festive as on a holiday!" Aviva said.

Ora came over and smoothed back the bright red hair. "You've slept through a dozen visitors, Malka told me. Adam and Moshe said they'll return."

And they did, each bringing a book and candy.

"I'll swell up and bust my cast!" Aviva laughed as she crammed chocolates into her mouth.

"You're thinner—but you look all right," Moshe said. "Ora said you'd had two operations."

Aviva explained the operations in great detail. "After they put my leg in a cast, they cut out this oblong window for observation which can be removed when the doctor needs to observe and is then fixed back in place with tape."

"Does it hurt when Erni treats it?"

"It's not exactly a pleasure."

"But why are the toes exposed?"

"It is a sort of indicator—if they become discolored—then I'm in trouble, but Erni is here, so I'm not worried."

"How long will you have the cast on?" Adam asked.

"Long enough—but it could have been worse."

The boys spoke of the three days of work with the Arabs. Moshe said, "No school for three days! A pleasure!"

"Fared's changed a lot," Adam offered. "It's as if he doesn't do things only for the show of it anymore. Remember how cocky he was, boasting about his car or his sports record? Remember how Laila stopped him with only a smile? Well, now it's as if the wind's been knocked out of him. He's changed."

Laila's changed me, too, Aviva reflected moodily. I want to be better than I am. Oh God, why did it have to happen to Laila?

Their solemn mood lasted until Moshe's restless eyes fell on the cookies. For once he had sufficient restraint to offer them to Aviva before seizing a handful.

"You've a new harmonica!" Aviva observed. The metal edge of it protruded from his shirt pocket.

"Adam gave it to me. His father sent it," Moshe said, handing her the instrument. "It's got scroll work engraved on it—something like my old one."

The knock was heard at the same time that the door opened, and Emmi and Avram came in. Avram looked critically at Aviva and said, "You don't look sick enough to be in bed!" and, laughing, ducked the book she aimed at him. Then he said something to Ora in a low voice and left. Would Erni come again that night? Aviva wondered. Not likely, not after her rudeness this morning.

"It looks very romantic with the two boys sitting on the floor at your feet," Emmi remarked.

"Any news of Yoram?" Aviva asked.

"He phoned and said the food in his unit is even worse than ours and, if it doesn't improve, they'll dump the cook on the Egyptians. He'll bring home two bags of dirty linen when he gets his first leave."

Just then Malka came in. Usually, her eyes held a lively twinkle, but now they were troubled, and she was breathing heavily. Ora, who had been listening to the softly tuned-in radio, looked at her questioningly.

"I just came from Amitai."

"In your condition you should not have climbed that steep hill!" Ora scolded. "Erni warned you about that!"

"But Amitai forgot his pills so I brought them. They're shelling Gan Shlomo," she said, lowering her voice.

"I just heard it over the radio."

Their voices were low, but Aviva heard about the shelling. Kibbutz Shlomo was only five miles to the north. Was theirs next? That night? The cottages on the lower level had shelters, but this lane had only trenches. Of course Avram or Erni would carry her to safety, but Avram was in charge of defense and Erni would be everywhere, should there be casualties.

She went numb with fear at the thought that she

would be trapped. And then she saw Moshe looking at her worriedly. He made himself useful by working in the fields, but she was utterly useless. The least she could do was to keep her fear secret.

Moshe said, "Vivi, should I play something?"

"Why not?" and suddenly, with the first lively notes of "Tzena, Tzena" she felt the tightness easing and began singing and clapping her hands to its beat.

Erni came in and she heard him tell Ora that Avram and Amitai had taken the fire-fighting equipment to Kibbutz Shlomo. Then he came over and ruffling her hair, said, "You sound like your jolly self again."

"You can't stay frightened all the time!" she said very gravely. "Erni, when we must go into the shelters, bring me to the children's. That way I can be of some use."

Erni nodded, thinking that, with these words, she had stopped being a child, and yet he felt she was still vulnerable in her new composure.

Later, when Ora had prepared her for sleep and was just about to turn off the lights, Aviva held out her arms to her. "*Imaleh*, I'll try to deserve being saved. I'll try to deserve you . . . everyone."

"Vivi, it is not too late to get you on a plane to New York—if we act quickly."

"But that was settled months ago! If I were in New York and read that there was shelling here—I would die of fear and shame."

"Why shame?"

"I could never come back here and look in the eyes of those who didn't run away."

Ora thought how strong a catalyst trouble was—it brought out the best and the worst in a person.

The first few days of June came, and each one ended as it began—with the same question in everyone's eyes. When will it begin?

The tempo in the *kibbutz* quickened. Everyone worked harder and faster. Leisure that first Sabbath in June brought no ease. And yet everyone was strangely calm, not just resigned, but with a pervasive sense that what will be, will be. Ora thought it wasn't fatalism, but a sort of grim acceptance.

Nobody said war, but everybody felt it would break out momentarily. The broadcasts from Cairo, from every Arab capital, vowed it hourly. In the north there was spasmodic shelling, and now and then Jordan spat fire at the southern *kibbutzim*. It was not altogether war, nor was it peace. The crisis dragged on.

We plan our lives in almost every detail and think we are in control of our destiny, Ora thought, but fate gives it a twist that tears it out of our hands. She lay staring in the darkening night and felt the futility of everything that they had worked for and suffered these many years, and she thought, "Why—and for how long—must we keep on paying a price for our existence?"

14

War!

As Ora approached the command bunker, early that Monday morning of June 5, 1967, Radio Kol Israel was flooding the air waves with the spirited theme song of "The Bridge on the River Kwai." It was followed by the battle hymn of the Israeli Armored Corps, and then a few lively Jewish folk songs were sung. Woven into the songs were the names of flowers and seemingly irrelevant words such as "alternating current," "good friends," "open windows." Ora knew these were code names for Israeli army units, and reservists belonging to them were being ordered to report at once for duty.

When she came into the bunker, Avram, Erni and Amitai stood huddled close to the radio. "It's begun!" Avram shouted at her.

". . . I repeat once, I repeat twice: Heavy

fighting has begun against Egyptian armor and aerial forces. . . ."

The tension that had been mounting these past few days suddenly eased and Ora felt a new strength.

At the news of the outbreak of war, officials of the *kibbutz* hurried into the bunker. Avram began briefing them on the plan of action that had already been drawn up: a detailed chart for defense, civilian and production tasks, with responsibility for each of these already assigned to the *kibbutzniks*.

"Anything overlooked?" Avram asked.

"Not overlooked, but not yet discussed," Ora said. "Should we evacuate the children? People have been telephoning from all over Israel, offering to take the children for safekeeping."

"How do our members feel about this?" Avram asked.

"A few mothers are undecided, but most of them are definitely against sending their children away," Ora replied.

"They are as safe here as in the towns," Emmi said. "Our shelters are very secure and comfortable."

Erni said, "Psychologically the children are better off here. Israel is so small that all of it is now the front line."

"I agree," Ora added. "It would be bad for the morale of our members, for people everywhere, if we sent the children away."

The *kibbutzniks* were leaving the bunker when two army officers entered, short, wiry, dark-skinned Mordecai, who was a captain in the Northern Command, and the other, Lieutenant Colonel Olek Posner, Adam's father. Olek Posner was a tall man of commanding appearance, with piercing eyes, a knife-edged nose and a whip scar, down the length of his right cheek giving his narrow face a hardness that vanished when he smiled.

"Olek! Did you drop out of the sky?" Ora asked, when both his hands closed over hers.

"Indeed we did!" he laughed. "By helicopter on your soccer field."

The *kibbutzniks* pressed around him, greeted him with affection and scolded him for the long absence since his last visit. He remembered all of their names, teased Amitai for subjecting everyone to American westerns, told Emmi that her son was well and itching to take on, single-handed, the entire Egyptian Army, and said to Erni, "Have I a girl for you—a real Negev beauty—she's a sergeant in . . ."

"Listen, matchmaker," Erni broke in laughingly. "If she's that beautiful, you would have married her yourself."

"True, but I have already made my choice," Olek replied with a glance at Ora.

Within a few minutes Posner lifted the spirit of the people so that, when they left the command bunker, their laughter echoed down the road.

Looking reflectively at Posner as he, Mordecai, Erni and Avram began discussing defense measures, Ora recalled a few personal items that appeared in a newspaper interview when he arrived in Israel over a year ago: ". . . a partisan at fifteen who fought the Nazis in the forests of Poland, a lieutenant in the Red Army at twenty, a student at the University of Warsaw after the war, and later a professor of economics there. He was appointed to the Polish

Economic Commission, then was entombed for seven years in a Polish prison and was eventually resurrected in Israel."

Her reflections were interrupted when Moshe and Adam ran breathlessly into the bunker. She looked questioningly from one to the other. Moshe could hardly contain his excitement as he gulped out, "We only now got word—we were in the orchard—yesterday Avram told us we're to be runners between the command bunker and the forward positions . . . he said to hold ourselves ready . . . and we're ready."

Adam paled and went rigid, when the tall officer turned from the wall map he was studying, and Adam saw he was his father.

"*Shalom,* Adam," his father said amiably.

Adam managed to breathe out a *shalom.* He quickened, took several long strides forward and was in his father's embrace. Then Posner stood him off and, with both hands on his shoulders, studied him. "You've grown a lot. How are you getting along?" he asked.

Erni frowned. The boy wasn't ready yet for paternal probing.

Instantly Adam thought of the trouble over the picture-taking, his unpopularity here and his face tightened. He shrugged and avoided his father's eyes.

"Would you like to share my room in Jerusalem?"

"Have there been complaints about me?" Adam asked.

"Should there have been?"

Adam crimsoned.

"No, there have been no complaints," his father said.

"Then why should I leave when I am needed here? I know very well how to use an Uzi."

Erni smiled. Ora, whose patience with the youth had long since worn thin, felt herself warming to him.

"Time to look at the top field," Mordecai reminded them, and Ora told the two boys to return later.

With a backward glance at his father, Adam followed Moshe out.

Malka, who was in charge of the army radio apparatus, and had been listening to the softly tuned-in transistor, now turned up the volume on the newscaster in Damascus and a high-pitched voice announced in Arabic: "Arabs, to arms! The hour of vengeance has come! We will meet in Tel Aviv! Strike with all your strength so that there will not remain any remembrance of the rabble on holy soil! On to Tel Aviv!"

"The empty vessel makes the greatest noise," Ora commented.

Amitai drove up in a truck and the two officers, with Ora, Avram and Erni, climbed on. They rode to the grazing pasture, past fields and orchards—beehives of activity with girls and boys at work. Avram led them past the zigzag trenches to the gun emplacements that were walled about with sandbags. The men in the dugouts called out a greeting to Posner, and he stopped to chat with them.

"Olek, is it deep enough?" asked one.

"Dig deeper," Posner replied. "Mother earth is

the best protection a soldier has," after which he and Mordecai went about examining the recently acquired mortars and artillery. Satisfied, they stood looking at the enemy position.

With the naked eye, they could see the gaping holes that were concrete bunkers, and dug into the flanks of the Syrian heights. Pillboxes rose in a zigzag up the escarpment, and in the bright morning sunshine they could see, beyond the glintings of barbed wire, the long steel barrel of their artillery.

When they returned from the command bunker, Malka said to Posner, "Olek, you're to call the area Military Command!" Then, after connecting him with headquarters, she said excitedly to Ora, "We've visitors! Arabs from Umm Tubas! They're waiting at the office. Khalil el Khoury and the *Mukhtar,* too!" Ora and Avram hurried out.

Awaiting them in his black limousine, Khalil fingered his beads nervously while the *Mukhtar* and a few Arab notables sat in solemn and reflective silence. Ibrahim Tabari, two of his sons, Fared, Adnan, and the youths of the work-study project stood grouped around three trucks and a tractor.

A quick glance told Ora that the men with Khalil were members of the Umm Tubas town council, and she felt apprehensive. They climbed out of the car and Avram welcomed them in Arabic as honored guests.

The *Mukhtar,* wearing a black-and-white checkered headdress and a dark jacket over pantaloons, was a short, paunchy man with a long nose that was spongy with pockmarks.

He said, "We Arab citizens of Israel are all

partners in the same fate. We are here to offer our help. We know you gave many of your trucks and tractors to the army. Use these we have brought for as long as you need them."

"We give you thanks from our hearts," Avram said. "But what if they are bombed and destroyed?"

Ibrahim, who had edged closer to his village officials, waited for their reply, and when they shrugged, he said, "Then we will all suffer together." Then, putting his hand on Avram's shoulder, he added, "We came to help. Use us where the need is greatest."

As he and the youths boarded the truck to the fields, Ora asked Khalil, "How is Abu Sa'id?"

"It was he who sent for the *Mukhtar* and proposed that we come to show our solidarity. Now I must return to him. Fared will bring back the car."

It had been a very long and exciting morning in the shelter and the children were becoming restless. They had already marveled over Aviva's plaster leg with its window, had already taken turns hopping around with her crutches, had already sung themselves hoarse with the songs they knew, had pushed crayons about on paper so that objects and animals and people of all sorts took shape, had already had their periods of ABC's and sums, and now, at supper, they were irritable and bored.

Was it really war at last? Aviva thought moodily. Was her mother safe in a bunker? Was Erni in the infirmary or in the forward posts? It was eerie being here, as if entombed in the depths of the earth, and not to know what was happening. Had Amitai gotten

all the cows down from the grazing field into the
sheds? She heard Emmi speaking softly to one of the
mothers, and she wondered how she could keep so
calm and efficient, knowing that Yoram was now in
battle.

When, later, the last of the fretful noises that
children make at bedtime subsided, Aviva picked up
her crutches to sit outside on the stairs.

Within a fuzzy circle of burnished gold, the sun
was beginning to dip into the horizon. A billowing
mass of clouds drifting over it took on opalescence
that tinted the top branches of the trees. It was all of
such peaceful grandeur that her eyes smarted at a
memory. It was at such an hour—not quite three
weeks ago—that Laila and she had watched the
pageant in the sky and revealed to each other their
innermost thoughts.

And, because one sorrow touches off memories
of still another sorrow, she thought of Yoram, Dudi
and all the youths and men of the *kibbutz* who, at
this very moment, were on the firing line. She froze
at the thought that the Arabs had one hundred
million persons on their side and they, the Israelis,
had none but themselves to rely on.

Questions surged in her mind: Why must there
be wars between people who were blood-related to
each other as were the Jews and Arabs? Why, when
Israeli land was only one percent of all the lands in
which Arabs lived did the Arabs fight to take it from
them? The refugees? Had not Israel absorbed the
same number of Arab Jews who had to flee Arab
countries? Why, if God promised them a return to

the land, did He place so many obstacles in their way?

She gave a start at the crunching sound of footsteps. Looking up, she saw four youths—Moshe, Adam, Fared and Adnan. She gave a joyful cry of welcome. It was as if they had materialized out of her need of them.

Fared looked emaciated, as if he had been feeding only on his sorrow. His skin was tightly drawn over his cheekbones and his eyes were sunk deep in their sockets. His hair was no longer pomaded and combed in tight waves, but was lusterless and rather untidy. There was a sad charm about him that moved Aviva, and she asked, "Fared, what have you been doing with yourself?"

"Working in the orchard until we were sent down to the bunker," he replied.

"How are you?" Adnan asked, as he descended the steps to sit beside her.

"Feeling useless," she said and shrugged. "Are you supposed to be out of the bunkers?"

"They didn't say we couldn't," Adam said. "The radios kept going all day, and they've gone potty in the bunker. They're reading the Bible and from it are mapping campaigns for the army!"

"Why not?" Moshe broke in. "We won great victories in those ancient days."

"Nearly two thousand years ago," Adam scoffed. "War now is technology and a good mechanic is worth . . ."

"A good mechanic is worth a whole Egyptian unit and our army consists mostly of mechanics,"

Moshe rebutted him. "I can take my Uzi gun apart and assemble it again in a few minutes."

"Don't boast," Aviva said dryly. "So can I. And Adam can, too." Then, turning to Fared, she asked, "Before today, what were you doing with yourself?"

"Nothing much. Reading a little." He was re-reading the books he had coasted through in high school, but which he now put his mind to. Nevertheless, war or no war, he had decided to work in the *kibbutz* even before the *Mukhtar* and the villagers had volunteered to help. It was his act of contrition for not informing on Abdul, who, in the last few days had vanished from the village.

"Mostly I take walks," he said aloud, and then added, "It helps me to think."

"Think about what?" Aviva asked. To her, a thinking Fared was an absolute contradiction, and inconsistent with the light-brained, carefree Fared she knew.

"I'm trying to decide what to do with my life."

"It's a problem?" Adam asked. "With all the wealth in your family?"

"Wealth has nothing to do with it," Fared said.

"What would you like to do?" Aviva asked, a little surprised but quite impressed with this serious-ness in him.

"That is exactly the problem. I thought I knew when I talked it over with Laila. But now I think I only said what would please her. Now I must decide for myself, and I'm not sure."

"You're nearly nineteen and you're not sure?" Moshe exclaimed. "I'm only sixteen and know definitely what I want to be! A pathologist." And, when Fared looked questioningly at him, he went on, "It's the field of medical science that deals with diseased conditions, their causes and nature."

Aviva smiled indulgently at him. A few months ago, he had been very excited about being a zoologist. In the lab and through a microscope, he had seen a whole world of living amoebae, in a drop of water, on a slide, and it had decided him for all time. And, of course, before that, he wanted to be a composer.

"I will be a psychiatrist," Adam announced.

"And I—." Aviva held back the words as if, now, it was an irrelevance. Aloud, she added, "I will go to the Teachers Seminary in Haifa. Working with children challenges the mind."

Fared looked from one to the other in awe. Here they were—the Children of Death his villagers had called them—sitting under the guns of the Syrians that would, maybe any minute, blast them out of existence. And they were thinking to the time ahead with total assurance that it belonged to them! He felt saddened by the thought.

It began to darken, although the sky still flamed with color. Aviva looked pensively at the dissolving clouds. The first day of war was ending, and they had been spared. Moshe's hand went to his pocket for his harmonica but with unhabitual shyness he refrained. Adam was describing the contest in the pear orchard over who would fill a basket first, which ended abruptly when they were summoned to the bunker. Then Moshe remembered the chocolate bar he had been saving all day for Aviva. He looked with dismay at the crushed and soggy mess that he took out of his pocket to offer her.

"Never mind, Moshele, it hasn't lost its sweetness," she said. "Have a lick, anyone?"

They all shook their heads.

It was two o'clock in the morning when those at the forward gun emplacements were relieved. Ora, who yawned and stretched with luxurious abandon, after four cramped hours of guard duty in the dugout, saw a figure emerging from out of the dark. Automatically she reached for her Uzi. A hoarse voice muttered the password. It was Erni.

Silently, they groped their way past the zigzag trenches to the hill road and, when the grazing pasture was above them, he asked, "Aviva all right?"

"Yes. The children quite adore her."

"News just came. We lost nineteen of ours but destroyed 374 enemy planes. In eighty minutes, in daylight, we destroyed Egypt's Air Force."

Ora caught her breath sharply. "I just can't believe it! How was this possible?"

"With skill and great courage," he said tiredly.

The trees were a solid mass of blackness against a murky, low-hanging sky. None of the buildings on the lower level were visible. It was as if the *kibbutz* had vanished.

"Want tea or a bite?" she asked when they reached their cottage.

"Neither. Sleep. Just sleep," he said and yawned as he lumbered up the stairs.

15

The Old Warrior

On the second morning of war, Adam and Moshe were on the way to the command bunker when they saw the plane low overhead.

"That's an Ilyushin 28, medium bomber," Adam said.

"How do you know?"

"Soviet. We had them in Poland."

In the bunker, Avram was discussing the work plans for the day with several men, while Olek Posner was drinking coffee as he listened to Radio Cairo: "Our glorious Arab army is about to enter Haifa. It is in flames."

"The glorious Arab army is still bogged down in the sands of Sinai," Posner said to Ora, as he poured a cup of coffee and handed it to her. Neither of them had yet had breakfast.

It was then that Moshe and Adam ran in with their news.

"How do you know it was a Soviet plane?" Posner asked Adam.

"I saw them at the air base in Warsaw," Adam said defensively. "I can tell the difference between Soviet planes and *ours!*"

Posner kept his smile inward as he lifted the special army telephone. His son had said "ours!"

It was quiet in the shelter, and Aviva relished her solitude as she occupied herself with cutting out paper letters for the kindergarteners. They had been taken by a few mothers for a quick bath. It had been a stormy morning; the four- and five-year-olds had been cranky and quarrelsome. They missed their playtime with their parents in the late afternoon hours, they missed the outdoors and hated being cooped up in one room for a second day. The novelty of being in the shelter had worn off, and it ceased being an adventure.

With a groan, Aviva set to work on the long-delayed letter to her father. She decided not to mention that she had been wounded, wondered what to write and found that she had really nothing to say to him.

Well, a beginning had to be made before the room became filled with the screechy little ones. She wrote:

Dear Paul, I am in the shelter listening to a radio broadcast of poetry written by kibbutz children. One by a ten-year-old, moved me so deeply that I am copying it for you.

The door was pushed open, and Emmi staggered in under the weight of a large, heavy box filled with fruit, cookies, piles of writing paper, books, boxes of crayons, topped by several chamber pots.

"You've cut your hair!" Aviva exclaimed, and gaped at Emmi as she unloaded the box on the table.

Smiling self-consciously, Emmi said, "The braids were too troublesome—I kept losing hairpins. Well, now it's less work."

Everything Emmi did she accomplished calmly, efficiently, but she had botched the haircutting. It was uneven. The right side was shorter than the left, and ragged at the nape of the neck. She looked younger but Aviva liked the old honey-colored coronet of braids infinitely more. There had been many changes in the *kibbutz* during her growing years, but Emmi's old-fashioned hairdo had been a constant. It was almost like losing a familiar landmark.

The haircut was very revealing, Aviva thought. Inside her shell of composure, Emmi must be frantic about Yoram. Everyone was nervous. It was evident in the sudden bursts of irrelevant chatter among the mothers in the shelter, words broken off at midsentence with a distant look, a sort of listening, waiting look that said, when? When will they shell us?

It was quiet that night when the children finally fell asleep, an uneasy sort of quiet and Aviva wished that someone would visit her. Earlier, her mother had dropped in briefly; last night she had come with Olek Posner, and it surprised Aviva how different he looked in uniform. Very commanding. He had complimented her on her bravery, and she had said, "I wasn't at all brave. I screamed terribly when it happened," and he said, "All soldiers, even the officers, know fear." He told her that, since his last visit, she had matured into a "young lady of real charm."

Why hadn't Erni ever complimented her?

She also noticed that when Posner and her mother left, he had put his hand on Ora's arm with a tenderness that was like a caress. Would Erni come tonight? It was three days since his last visit. Didn't he even concern himself about her as a patient?

She wished that Moshe would come. She'd ask him to play the piece he had composed, especially for her, when she danced at the Independence Day festivities. He never had to be coaxed to play, and he had an extraordinary range of songs.

Were Fared and Adnan still in the *kibbutz?*

It was all very wearying. And the quiet seemed so unnatural. Frightening, too.

When?

Late that night, as she drifted into sleep, Ora heard, as from a great distance, the ringing of the telephone. Switching on the light, she reached for the instrument, then realized that it sounded from the room above hers—Erni's. It rang insistently. He must be drugged with exhaustion, as she was. There had been accidents in the orchards, ugly bruises he had to attend to, and deep cuts. He had performed minor surgery. Some persons had come to the infirmary complaining of pains which he diagnosed as nerves. The premature birth of a baby had kept him tied to the mother's bedside, sweating out the ordeal of possible death and, finally, the birth.

Ora rose to wake him when the ringing ceased, and she heard his voice answering sleepily.

A minute later as he came vaulting down the stairs with his medical case, Ora saw that his face was unshaved and puffy from lack of sleep. Like her, he had gone to bed fully dressed. She stood at her door with a questioning look.

"Khalil phoned. It's Abu Sa'id."

"I'll go, too. Shall we take Fared?"

"Yes, fetch him. I'll get the truck."

"Use Khalil's car. The keys are in the side compartment."

With all the lights out, the night was unfriendly and somewhat eerie. The western *kibbutzim* that always threw golden spears of light across the hills were blacked out, too, and, like Tel Hashava, had been absorbed into the darkness between earth and sky.

"May I drive?" Fared asked.

"No," Erni said gruffly. "I've been with you at the wheel and only a miracle brought me safely home."

Silently, they moved downhill into layers of a deeper blackness, but Erni's unerring instinct kept them on the road. Umm Tubas had blended into the night, and only the slender white tower of the mosque, like a warning finger pointing skyward, told them they were in the Arab village.

"Ora, did she—Laila—know that I had telephoned?"

"Yes, Fared. I told her a few minutes before the mine exploded. I think it was the last thing she really heard, because the joy of it was on her face when she died."

Fared touched her arm in gratitude.

Here and there, the darkness was slashed by the white cubes of houses, but the large el Khoury house sat like a massive jeweled crown on the hill, with only one hooded light at the terrace. Khalil stood waiting for them and, wordlessly, he led them to the Old Warrior's room.

Even before Erni spoke, even before the wailing broke out somewhere in the house, Ora knew that Abu Sa'id was dead. He had the same look of expectancy that Noah had had in his last moment, a sort of unfinished smile, as if he were experiencing some sort of wonder and was about to remark on it when breath left him. So, too, had been Noah's last smile.

Noah and Abu Sa'id. As alike as two grains of wheat.

With their reason and their compassion, they sowed peace in the hearts of people. But now these two deaths stabbed at a nearer and deeper pain, and she felt sick with the awareness of loss. She had lost the two men to whom she had always been a child, and suddenly she felt old and alone and a little frightened.

On Wednesday, the third day of war, the *kibbutz* stirred to life before dawn and, somberly, the people glimpsed a leaden sky into which the sun had not yet edged itself. They had slept fitfully, momentarily expecting the summons to the bunkers. They rose, faces drawn and heavy-eyed, to a day of grueling tasks and anxieties, which soon worsened at the news of Abu Sa'id's death and the broadcast by Kol Israel: heavy fighting continued in Jerusalem.

As the morning wore on, no further news of Jerusalem's fate came through. The smoke of burning fields spiraled up from neighboring *kibbutzim,* as news of the death of Abu Sa'id spread. The Arabs of Umm Tubas failed to appear, and the *kibbutzniks* were seized by an old but recurring fear—if the Syrians invaded, to whom would the Israeli-Arabs be loyal, now that Abu Sa'id was no longer alive to reason with them?

When?

Coming down from the old military field, Avram saw people rushing to the command bunker and heard the commotion before he reached them. They stopped him with shouts, "Avram! Is it true? Our radio sputtered. . . ." Avram ran inside the bunker, and even Posner's voice at the telephone had this tense uncertainty. He made gestures with his free hand for silence. Then he put down the telephone and turned the radio on full strength.

"Jerusalem is ours! I say it twice, Jerusalem is ours! The west wall of our holy Temple is now in our hands!"

Now the first note of the *shofar* sounded, that awesome, throbbing sound of the ram's horn used from the start of their nationhood on the high holidays and in time of war. And, as the rabbi at the wall offered the prayer that blessed God "Who has kept us in life and preserved us and brought us to this day," all in the bunker responded with a hearty "Amen!"

Dabbing at her eyes, Ora asked Posner, "Why am I weeping when I am not religious?"

Posner said, "Because that wall—that remnant of our Temple—is the symbol of our ancient nationhood—and our continuity."

That night, it was announced over the radio that Egypt and Jordan had requested a cease-fire. Moshe and Adam were in hot disagreement over it. Still arguing the matter, they came to Aviva's shelter and, on their latticed hands, they brought her into the fresh evening air and sat her down on the top stair.

"If we accept the cease-fire, nothing will change," Moshe said, renewing the argument. "The Syrians will still be shelling down on us."

"Either you trust the United Nations or . . ." Adam started to say when Moshe, his voice high with outrage, broke in with, "Trust them when they gave the go ahead to Nasser by pulling out the U.N. forces at Sharm-el-Sheik . . . don't you wave that U.N. flag at me!"

"But isn't it better to have a cease-fire now—before the Syrians shell us?" Adam asked. "Kibbutz Shlomo is still burning. . . ."

"No! I say, no!" Moshe cried out, anguished. "Did you hear our people in the bunkers? They want the army to go up those hills—the *kibbutzim* are sending a delegation to Eshkol demanding this—Erni and Ora went with them. And if the government won't agree to it, we'll go up there ourselves and rip out those guns."

"No one can climb Golan Heights with heavy guns!" Adam said.

"Yes, they can!" Aviva insisted. "We can't let them stay up there shooting down at us. We can't end the war by letting things remain as they were!"

"But if there is a demilitarized zone . . . ," Adam said doggedly.

Aviva and Moshe exchanged glances, as of some shared memory, and then she said, "That military zone never stopped them from coming right into the *kibbutz* to lay mines—to steal our cows. Moshe's father was killed by Syrian gunfire near that zone, on our own side! He'd gone after a cow that had strayed close to the zone."

Quietly now, Moshe said, "My father used to watch the goats up there. He saw their hoof marks as they climbed. He said one day he would climb up with a mortar and wipe out those murdering bandits. Well, he can't, but I will. Yes, I will lead our army up those goat tracks . . . you believe me, Vivi, don't you?"

"Yes, Moshe, I believe you," she said, and leaning over, she kissed him.

16

A Young Defender Falls

On Thursday before dawn, the fourth day of war, a shell streaked through the air over the grazing field. It landed on the parapet of sandbags at Amitai's gun emplacement and sent up a geyser of earth that nearly buried him. Stunned for a moment, he worked frantically to free himself and dug out the telephone. He spoke urgently into it, then repeated his message. There was no response at the other end.

In the command bunker, Avram said to Ora, "That shell sounded close," and connected himself with the forward position. "Avram here. Do you hear me? Avram here." The wire at the other end was dead.

Ora sounded the alarm, and the siren rang through the lower *kibbutz*. It brought Moshe and Adam running to the command bunker.

"Moshe, get to Amitai. Fast! Tell him not to fire until they fire again," and to Adam, who carried one shoe which he was trying to put on, "Run to the new orchard—the wire's down. Tell everyone to get into the bunkers."

When Adam finally got his shoe on and ran out, Moshe was out of sight on the curved hill road. Here the siren was only a faint sound. Adam had already gone past the first level of orchards, when a sudden whistling rush of air pressed against his ears and he lurched forward. Something flashed high above him and, splitting into fiery fragments, dropped into a nearby field. The earth growled and seemed to shift under his feet. His heart pounded and he felt as if his lungs were bursting.

Should he go on? The wail of the siren was fainter here, but surely the workers would hear it and run into the deep trenches around the orchard. He was a mass of quivering nerves, and sweat oozed down his face. Adam felt mortified at his cowardice. Then, with a stifled sob, he ran on.

He was within sight of the higher orchard and was already yelling out his message to the workers, when a truck with Avram and a few others careened past him. Avram yelled at him to get into a trench.

Had Moshe reached the grazing pasture?

Moshe climbed a straight course through the rows of saplings. Elated, he cried out, "It's begun! Now we'll pay them back! Now!"

Earlier, in the bunker, no one had been frightened at the first shell. Not one! The tension broke— at last they were sharing the war with the border *kibbutzim!* A tough courage passed from one to the other.

His *chaverim!* Moshe loved them all. Adam, too. Adam racing him to the command bunker, one shoe in his hand. He laughed at the comic picture he made, and the sound of his laughter seemed to outrun him so that it greeted him at the alfalfa field when he reached it. Clouds of bees were feeding on the purple flowers. Oh, but they would have plenty of honey this fall!

A whistling rush of sound tore over his head and a flare burst into the air. It fragmented into rosettes of flames. One of them struck him, and it felt like knives stabbing at him.

At one o'clock that afternoon, the shelling stopped. In the command bunker, Ora pressed her hands to her ears but the roaring persisted. Throughout the morning, the office switchboard was busy with calls from distant *kibbutzim,* offering to take the children. Parents, relatives, friends in the towns insisted on speaking to Ora and she had said so often, "Thank you, but they are safe in our underground shelters" that she felt the words would come automatically to her lips, no matter what the question. Spent with fatigue, she slumped deep in her chair. Had the shelling really stopped?

The quiet lengthened, and then, suddenly, she roused herself and ran out of the bunker toward the children's section. Already the women were climbing to the upper trenches with hot food for the workers.

She stopped with a cry. A red haze hung over the alfalfa field and the orchards. Their crops were ruined. But the truck with the fire-fighting equipment was already on its way. In the three warehouses in which grain and fodder were stored, flames and smoke poured out and only a trickle of water dripped from the hoses. Had the shelling destroyed their main water tank?

Farther along, the dining hall stood intact, but the front windows lay splintered on the ground. The roof of a cottage was cracked open, and a door swung and sagged away from its hinges. The wall of the end cottage was split down the middle. She ran to the children's shelter.

Aviva and the children were napping, and a few mothers stood about talking softly. Haggard with strain, Emmi stopped washing the dishes and smiled wanly at Ora.

"Everyone all right?" Ora asked. When Emmi told her how well everyone had behaved during the shelling, Ora stopped her in midsentence. "Tell Vivi I was here," and she hurried out.

She heard a crackle of shots and stood still to determine its direction. It sounded close, and seemed to come from the area of the cow barns. She ran to where a crowd stood at the fenced-off yards, and pushed through to the fence. Amitai was shooting the cows lying at the edge of a crater in the yard.

"Stop him! He's killing our cows!" a woman cried as she seized Ora's arm.

"He has to—they're wounded," Ora replied as she swung herself over the fence. She moved toward Amitai, but stopped when she saw his anguished face, as he stood with a rifle over a cow lying on her side, her soft brown eyes fixed beseechingly on him, her teats oozing blood. He fired, and swearing obscenely, turned away.

Wordlessly, Ora moved past him to the bombed-out barn. Men were hosing down the cement floor, and the water ran the blood into the yard.

"We've lost twenty cows," one of the workers said to her.

As she returned to the command bunker, Adam came running toward her. "I can't find Moshe anywhere. As soon as the shelling stopped, I looked for him everywhere." He followed her inside.

Avram was at the telephone, and when he finished he yawned and said tiredly, "That was the Northern Command. The army will be here early in the morning."

"Good! Have you seen Moshe?"

"No. And he didn't get up to the grazing field with my message either."

"I can't find him!" Adam cried. "Something has happened to him!"

"Have you looked at the upper orchards? He might have started working when the shelling stopped.

"I looked there."

Just then, a man in wet, smoky clothes came in, nodded Avram aside and whispered something. Avram looked startled. "If it's so burned, how do you know it is Moshe?"

The worker looked nervously at Ora, frowned as if weighing a thought, and then said, "The harmonica and his glasses were on the ground beside him."

"Oh my God!" Ora gasped.

"It's my fault! I said it was faster climbing up through the orchards . . . ," Adam said, and dropped his face into his hands.

In the shelter, the mothers were preparing the children for bed. It was much earlier than their accustomed time, but the nerve-shattering day that had begun at dawn, now seemed endless to the children, and they were too fatigued even for the usual bedtime stalling. But the undressing and stand-up washing dragged on and frayed Aviva's nerves. Tension had been mounting inside her all that afternoon. She wanted to go outside to see what had happened in the *kibbutz,* but Ora, in her brief visit while she had napped, left orders that no one except Emmi and the mothers were to leave the shelter until notified. Had anyone been killed or wounded, were any houses destroyed? She had a foreboding of some terrible disaster. The suspense of not knowing made her tense all afternoon, though she had forced herself to be cheerful lest the children sense her distress and become nervous, too.

Emmi knew something, she felt certain. Her face looked drained and her eyes were red-rimmed. She broke dishes and listened absently when anyone spoke to her. Aviva felt if she could only go outdoors and smell the fresh air and just move about to see with her own eyes.

It seemed to her as if the children, after being docile about going to bed, after their wash-up, had been somehow recharged—and had become lively again. She was about to snap at Rina when the door opened. It was Erni! She started to get up but fell back and felt the tears starting. He leaned down, kissed her and held her close.

"Erni! Erni!" The children tugged at his sleeve, clamoring to be noticed.

"Is—everything ready?" Emmi asked him as she took off her smock. He nodded as he bent to pat a child, tousle another's hair. He picked up Aviva's crutches and handed them to her, saying, "We are going for a short ride."

Outside, she drew in long breaths of air and then her eyes widened—the flowering tops of the jacaranda tree had been lopped off in the shelling!

"Have you been okay?" Erni asked as they began climbing.

"Yes," she lied. The tension all day had settled in her leg and pained unbearably. "See how easily I move on my four legs?" and she swung herself forward on her crutches.

The el Khoury limousine stood a short distance away, and behind it a caravan of three trucks. Fared was at the wheel of his family's car and he gave her his sad smile. The *Mukhtar* of Umm Tubas sat solemn faced beside him. In the rear sat Ora, Avram and the white-bearded rabbi, from their neighboring orthodox *kibbutz,* who came here to perform marriages or to pray at funerals. Abstractedly, Aviva thought that he wore the same long, black caftan and black satin, fur-trimmed hat for either occasion.

Where were they going?

In the first of the three trucks stood some of the boys and girls of the *kibbutz*. Ibrahim was at the wheel and, between him and Adnan, sat Adam, whose eyes were swollen and red.

Her blood froze. Somehow she knew but she resisted the knowledge, as if just thinking about it would make it true and irrevocable. She rasped out, "Where are we going?"

"To a funeral," Erni replied.

"Moshe?"

He nodded.

She felt nothing, neither pain nor sorrow, merely a sudden weightlessness. She could not move, and Erni lifted her into the car. Avram pulled down the jump seats and he, Erni and Emmi sat facing her.

They were silent as the car started to climb and then Ora said, "Vivi, tomorrow morning our army will come here . . . our friends from Umm Tubas brought food . . . they thought our kitchen had been shelled. They offered to help us rebuild. Many *kibbutzim* telephoned to ask what we needed."

Aviva heard the flow of words but they bounced off her mind without impact. She was locked in her own thoughts; Laila . . . Moshe. They passed a row of cottages, and she saw cracks in walls and a large hole which a climbing bougainvillaea failed to cover. They came to the orchards, and the acrid smell of smoke rasped her throat. Already the higher alfalfa field was crowned with clusters of purple flowers and swarms of bees were hovering over them. There would be plenty of honey . . . Moshe loved honey . . . she thought if she could cry, it would ease the burning in her eyes.

The cemetery lay across a slope on the western side of the *kibbutz*. Ora walked along a gravel path marked on both sides with small yellowish marble tombstones that summoned up a face, a comrade who had those many years ago labored with her breaking the clayey, unyielding earth for their first planting. Shlomo, the father of Moshe, lay here. And it came to her that of the twenty buried here, nine had been killed by Syrian mines or snipers. Yes, the land had been dearly bought and paid for with their lives.

Already a fuzz of green had speared through Noah's grave and, with a wry smile, she thought of putting a teakettle on it as he had teasingly requested.

Now the mourners ranged themselves around the freshly made grave. Eight boys brought the coffin and placed it on ropes at its edge.

As Amitai and Avram began lowering it, Aviva suddenly lurched forward, her hand thrust out to stop them. "Why are you rushing it? Why?" she asked.

"Because tomorrow we may be bombed again," Ora said.

"But I want to see him! I must tell him . . ." and stopped. Erni had put his arm around her shoulders.

The old rabbi began intoning the ancient prayer: *El Mahleh Rahamin!"*

As they began shoveling earth over the coffin, Emmi began to sob. Dry-eyed, Ora wondered who among them would next pay with his life, so that Israel could live.

Across from her, at the other end of the grave, Aviva saw Adam hunched over, with Adnan and Fared on either side of him. His lips were clenched together but his chin quivered. Her eyes, riveted to him, forced him to meet hers, and they locked in a long unwavering stare. Did he remember how he used to torment Moshe? Adam seemed to shrink into himself as he looked away.

The rabbi ended the rites with the "dust to dust" prayer, and the mourners began moving away from the grave. Aviva stood where she was, her eyes fixed on the mound under which Moshe lay, and she took a few steps closer. Bending down, she removed a few small stones and smoothed out the uneven earth with the palm of her hand. Softly she said, "Moshe, my friend, my *chaver*. Moshele. Tomorrow when the army comes, you will lead them up the goat path. With one hand you will play your harmonica and wave on our defenders with the other. I will watch you climb those hills. Moshele."

17

The Lights Go On!

Early Friday morning, the fifth day of war, the settlers turned on their radios and heard that the Syrian Minister for Foreign Affairs had cabled Secretary General U Thant at the United Nations, accepting his call for a cease-fire.

It was as if a bombshell had exploded in their midst. A cease-fire would leave the Syrians in their hill-top posts with guns still aimed at the *kibbutzim.*

In the command bunker, after listening to this broadcast, Ora switched to the Syrian radio in Damascus: ". . . the campaign continues! It will not end until after we have raised our Palestinian flag in the skies of Tel Aviv! Continue your war against the enemy, kill his men and his units, fight a total war! We will meet in Tel Aviv! We will meet in Tel Aviv!

194

Palestine *fedayeen!* Strike! Destroy! Explode! Act now! Act now, and do not hesitate!"

The Northern Command telephone rang and, answering it, Ora heard, "The Syrians have now launched a massive artillery attack on the four *kibbutzim* in the lower area."

"But the U.N. has just announced the Syrian cease-fire!"

"We heard it too. But the Syrians can't break an old habit. Be prepared and on the alert . . . hold on."

A vigorous bass voice spoke, "Deborah?" (This was her code name, and it had flattered her that they had chosen to call her after their biblical warrior prophetess.) It was Olek Posner, and she quickened at the sound of his voice. "How goes it?"

"Morale high. We are ready and waiting."

"Good! *Chazak v'amots!*" had replaced "*shalom!*" when signing off.

The nudge on his shoulder woke Adam. Startled, he came alert and reached for the Uzi gun slung over his shoulder. He had been on guard duty in the trench all night. He felt certain he had been awake throughout and had not dozed off but merely closed his eyes. He felt chagrined as the pretty *chavera* smiled down at him. The sun was only a pale arc edging into the sky, and here she was, and others with her, fresh-looking and cheerful, serving a breakfast of hot, sugared coffee and thick slices of bread spread with jam.

He was famished. He hadn't eaten since breakfast yesterday, his fast was an act of contrition for all the trouble he had given Moshe. Drinking his coffee, he watched the young women pushing the conveyor of food to the orchard where the *kibbutzniks* were already at work. Their exchange of banter was pleasant-sounding and reassuring in the early morning air. It was as if things were normal again.

Continuing the questions that had kept him alert during the night, he wondered why he had felt a vast distaste for these settlers. When he had come here, he thought that they were inferior to the Poles, and he thought, too, the way they held themselves with a superior air was ridiculous when they were only peasants!

Mingling with them in the orchards these past few weeks, sweating to pick the fruit before it rotted in the hot sun, on guard with them, he had allowed himself to know them, and now he felt better about living here.

Brought up an atheist, Adam could not understand man's compelling need for a faith that had hope as its core. "Hope *and* work make our *kibbutzim* flourish" Ora had said in one of her work-study lectures. A few days ago, he and Moshe had helped with the wheat harvesting and, before setting the machine in motion, the tractor driver offered a prayer, "Bless this year unto us, together with every kind of the produce thereof for our welfare, give blessing upon the face of the earth . . ." and it had struck Adam that the *kibbutznik* had prayed for a good harvest, not only for themselves, but for all on the face of the earth!

All during last night he had kept awake, asking himself some probing questions. He now felt that he had disliked Moshe from the beginning because he was Aviva's pet and because the settlers pampered him with love. He thought it had been contempt he had felt for him, but now he knew that it had been jealousy.

Did they wish that it had been he, and not Moshe, who had been killed? He had wanted to throw the harmonica into the grave before Moshe was lowered into it, but just that instant he caught Aviva staring at him, with such aversion, that he felt certain she wished that it was he, instead of Moshe, who was being buried.

"Adam! Go to a bunker and sleep! And don't you spend another full night on guard duty! Dead heroes are no use to us!"

It was Ora—and she was scolding him affectionately! She was concerned about him! How did she know that he had come here immediately after the funeral and remained all night? With a chuckle, he vaulted out of the trench and stumbled over the strap of his Uzi gun.

He barely made it to the bunker before the shelling began again.

Ora went through the village to assay the new damages. She heard the rumble of vehicles before she saw them and then, all at once, the *kibbutz* road as far down as Umm Tubas was a moving line of bulldozers, tanks, tractors, half-tracks, jeeps, public buses and commercial trucks with the names of the owners still on them. The army had come!

Emerging from their bunkers, the people stared in disbelief and then bolted forward to welcome the soldiers with roars of *shaloms,* reaching out to seize a hand and pat a shoulder. Slowly, the transport rolled on in unending numbers and, watching, Emmi stopped scanning faces to remark to Ora, "Look at all those trucks! It's hard to believe our army had so many!"

"Why not? They've most of ours!" Ora said.

And then a stocky youth, his red beret perched at an angle on his thick brown hair, leaped down from a jeep, scrambled toward Emmi and seizing her, swung her off the ground in a wild embrace.

"Yoram!" Emmi wailed. "But you've gotten so thin!"

"I feel better this way," Yoram said and grinned. "How is *Abba?* Everybody?" and stopped with a low whistle as his glance took in a roofless building, a jagged strip of wall.

"Your father is well—everybody is," Emmi said, noticing that her son had achieved a sergeant's stripe.

"Are Fared—Adnan—the others—still here?" he asked.

"They were," Ora replied. "We told them to stay home when the shelling began the other day. And Ibrahim and the others let us have their trucks and a tractor and yesterday, after the shelling stopped, they brought food. They said that volunteers will help us rebuild as soon as . . ." and she smiled away the rest.

Now more settlers came, bringing baskets of fruit, cookies, bottles of soda pop and, moving alongside the vehicles, thrust them into outstretched hands. Youngsters swarmed around the transport, climbed onto tanks and sat astride them, fancying themselves to be mascots. The soldiers held out slips of paper with telephone numbers, "Call my parents." "Tell my wife hello, from Shuly!" "Be sure you tell my mother you saw me!" "Tell Dan—he's my kid brother—we're settling accounts for good!"

"I've got to run!" Yoram said, as the transport, which had slowed to a standstill, began inching along. And then he gaped at his mother's hair. "*Ima!* You've cut it!"

Emmi's smile faded. "Don't you like it? I've still got the braids, . . ." her voice trailed away unhappily.

"It's not bad. In fact, well, never mind, it's okay. Tell Vivi you saw me," and saying that he loped up the road toward a bus from which red berets were waved at him.

"He got so thin," Emmi sighed, to which Ora observed, "Did you notice how clear his skin is now?" and she began moving about to collect the slips of papers. The switchboard would be kept busy all day with the messages from the soldiers.

Suddenly, with a roar and a great rush of wind, Israeli planes streaked overhead to the Syrian hills, drowning out the cheers and the wildly joyful shouts from the *kibbutz.*

There was a great stir of activity in the two rooms of the children's shelter. The older ones had put aside their studies and drawings, their knitting and their books, and busied themselves cleaning the room for the *Shabbat.*

The smaller ones fussed with their bedding,

shook out the dirt that had dropped from the ceiling with each shelling, smoothed out blankets and tucked their pajamas under their pillows. The mothers busied themselves with the heavier chores of scrubbing, sweeping and setting things in order. War or no war—the *Shabbat* had to be welcomed properly.

Earlier, there had been fist fights between several of the boys in the "seniors" room, and a hair-pulling and face-scratching among the smaller children. But when Emmi brought news that the army, on its way to the Golan Heights, would pass through Tel Hashava, it was as if she had said that God would pass through the *kibbutz,* and an awed hush settled on the shelter. And then everyone fell to their tasks with a zeal never before brought to their efforts.

Everyone but Rina. She lay on her bunk, eyes shut, face grim and deep in the process of a think-out. Aviva braced herself for trouble. Then, with a sweetness in her tone that augured even more trouble than Aviva anticipated, Rina said, "My daddy is a general, almost. . . ."

"Your daddy is not a general, not even almost, but a sergeant, same as Yoram," Aviva quickly interjected, knowing that to spike one of Rina's wild exaggerations was certain to diminish her demands.

But Rina was not discouraged.

"And my mommy saves the soldiers when they get hurt. . . ."

"That is true," Aviva admitted warily.

"They want to see me, so I will go up to the fields to pick flowers for them, and then I will go down to wait for them at the road into our *kibbutz!"*

With a toss of her black curls she sat up, chin fisted, arms crossed and defied Aviva—or anyone else—to thwart her will.

Aviva, who had plans of her own and felt guilty about denying to Rina what she herself intended to do, said matter-of-factly, "No one but our defenders are allowed up on the old military field, and no one leaves the shelter until we get word to do so."

The children crowded around her, demanding to see the soldiers.

"They are not here yet, and they will say what a bad lot you are not staying in shelters, but getting in their way when they are coming to defend you. Now, let's suppose!"

"Let's suppose!" the children shouted back gleefully. Aviva knew many more exciting games than their real teacher did.

"Let's suppose God was to grant you one wish—what would you most wish for?"

"My daddy to come home!" shrilled out a chorus.

". . . and?" Aviva prompted.

"That the Arabs stop shelling!"

"That there be peace!"

"That the Western Wall be ours for ever and ever!"

"That they won't bomb houses, so we don't ever have to live in shelters again!"

"That the Arabs think it is better to live in peace, so they won't take our land. We need it, too, and we'll send them flowers."

They squealed with delight when Aviva called out a second round of wishes and, remembering the panic in these eyes yesterday, she thought that either they had become inured to the roar of the shelling—or their need to imagine they were secure transcended their fears.

Several hours later, when the soldiers came and permission was given to the children to leave the shelter, they erupted full-throated into the dazzling sunshine.

Like eagles alighting, helicopters swooped down on the sports field and disgorged company after company of paratroopers who were to spearhead the assault on the Syrian hills. The military transport had reached the grazing plateau, and a bulldozer was already clawing a road out of the hills with a full column of armor in its wake.

Earlier, Israeli planes had looped around the escarpment dropping bombs. The settlers on the old military field stood watching, heard blast after blast and cried out with awe each time a gray cloud mushroomed skyward. The ground vibrated under the watchers from the exploding shells. Smoke billowed up and covered the Syrian village across them like a shroud. Tanks began inching their way up the escarpment; the ground forces followed.

Leaning forward on her crutches, Aviva saw in her mind's eye a slight, bespectacled youth in the forefront, climbing as sure-footed as a goat, his Uzi gun waving onward those behind him while he piped away on his harmonica. And the soldiers followed the trail he made.

Then, suddenly, moving black dots that were Syrian planes plummeted out of the sky to stitch mantles of fire over the lower hillsides. Israeli tanks burst into flames and armored cars heaved up and turned over, but the troops on wheels and those on foot continued their relentless crawl upward. The Syrian planes vanished.

It was not yet dusk when the blue and white Israeli flag was raised on the topmost post of the Syrian hills. In the north, orange flares lit up the sky and the sound of gunfire could still be faintly heard.

The settlers began drifting down to the dwellings to welcome the *Shabbat*. They walked without speaking, with only the shuffling of their footsteps breaking the silence of the gathering night. They felt too drained with the tensions and the heavy work to gloat over the victory.

They would not feel secure until the last gun went silent, and would not rejoice until the last of the defenders returned home.

On Saturday, June 10, the sixth day of war, at 6:30 P.M., all the guns along the Syrian front were silenced.

Several hours later, as the youth of the *kibbutz* were clearing away the rubble on the sports field, a helicopter touched down. The boys and girls held back, uncertain, but when a few paratroopers and Lieutenant Colonel Posner emerged, they ran toward them shouting, "Yoram! Shuly! Dan! Tal." The soldiers were surrounded and wildly embraced.

Posner saw his son piling broken slabs of cement on a wheelbarrow, saw him take a hesitant step toward him and then come running into his arms.

Aviva had never seen Ora's room so crowded and lively with talk. People kept coming and going as if only in movement could they contain their excitement. Yoram was home—and the safe return of a son of the *kibbutz* was a rejoicing for all.

With Erni's arm around her, Aviva thought that perhaps all this was only a dream, the kind she went to sleep on, when she fixed her mind on two thoughts and passionately *willed* them to happen; that the war be quickly over and won, and that Erni come and kiss her on the mouth and take her in his arms. Yes, the war was over and won, and here she was in Erni's arms!

And everyone who mattered most in her life was safe and in the room: Erni, Ora, Yoram, Avram, Amitai, Malka and even Adam! If only Laila and Moshe were here. . . .

Emmi, her braided coronet fastened back into place with hairpins, kept one eye on the teakettle and another on her son, who was telling them all that he had seen, heard and done these past two climactic days on the Syrian heights.

". . . and over their radio we heard the Russians instructing the Syrians in Russian, and in the bunkers we saw pictures of Russian instructors with Syrian officers and military manuals and technical guides— all in Russian!"

Ora glanced questioningly at Posner. He nodded. "I heard them when we monitored their communications, and I speak Russian." Then he gave his deep roar of a laugh. "At the end I heard one of the Russians saying: 'The blacks are running—the Jews are coming.' "

"But the Syrians were good fighters," Yoram said. "They are taught that hatred is sacred, and they fought like lions with their rifle butts, knives, fists, even with their teeth!"

As he spoke, Ora looked reflectively at him and felt pride in him. He was praising, not hating, the enemy, and this was good.

In the midst of the talk, Amitai broke in with a snort of impatience, "So now that we are on top of the heights, what will happen if the U.N. tells us we must go back to being sitting ducks—as if we lost the war?"

All eyes focused on Posner, who shrugged in that age-old Hebraic gesture of doubt that hinted of hope. "The Soviets will see to it that we make no gains out of our victory. We must look only to ourselves to guarantee our own security—but we must strive as hard to make peace as we strove for victory, because war breeds war."

War breeds war. His words touched off troubled thoughts in Aviva. Will we always live in a state of siege? Did it mean that there was small hope for a normal state of existence? Did it mean that we must concentrate on developing a military mentality at the expense of the artistic, the philosophic?

War breeds war. Ora wondered if there would ever be peace in the land, the kind of peace that could narrow one's horizon to one's personal problems, without qualms that something for the *kibbutz* was being left undone? Last month she had said to her work-study study group, "Our foreign policy is simple—it is to live and let live! Peace!" And now Posner said war breeds war. When will this vicious cycle end? She rose to help Emmi serve tea. But Emmi had forgotten to turn on the electricity under the teakettle and Ora came back into the room. Everyone was listening raptly to Posner.

". . . and one of the ironies of life here in Israel is that, if you want peace, you have to prove you can fight. Maybe one day the Arabs will come to terms with the fact that we can fight. During the war with the Germans the Allies decided that there would be no compromise with the total evil that was Hitlerism. So when we defeated the Nazis, we totally occupied Germany.

"Here, our Southern Command could have occupied all Egypt, our Central Command could have taken all Jordan and our Northern Command was only forty miles from Damascus. But we stopped when we did—not only because of the cease-fire— but because we believe it is possible to negotiate and compromise with the Arabs."

He was silent a moment, pulled reflectively at his ear, and then added, "When I was with the Jewish partisans fighting the Nazis, we lost many men not only because we were poorly equipped but because the Poles betrayed us to them. Here, we were worried about the Israeli-Arabs—on whose side would they be when war broke out—and they proved to be loyal to us. This is something to remember."

"Indeed it is!" Ora exclaimed, when she saw the chagrined look on Amitai's face. "That first day of war our Arab neighbors came to us with their *Mukhtar* and said, 'we are all Israelis!' They offered us their trucks and, when Avram warned that they might be destroyed in the shelling, Ibrahim Tabari said 'then we will all suffer together.' And before that it was Laila, his daughter, who said, 'war between Jews and Arabs is fratricide—we are of one family.' "

A pensive look came over Aviva's face as she listened, and she thought of the volunteers from Umm Tubas who were coming tomorrow to help rebuild; she thought of Adnan, the gentle poet of peace, and she thought of Fared, who was still in search of himself.

She thought back of the day, only four months ago, when she had read her father's letter, and she had brought her problem to the old military field. Had she really even considered leaving the *kibbutz* for safety in New York?

They had suffered a war and, throughout the shelling, she had not once felt the fear that had seized her that day on the military field. She had felt no fear because the others in the *kibbutz* had been so strong, and this had strengthened her. She hoped she would prove herself deserving. Hope, she knew, was not enough, but you cannot do anything meaningful without it.

She felt so good about this that, in an access of joy, she rose and turned to the window. She cried out, "Oh! Look!"

All the lights were springing on in the Galilee *kibbutzim!*

About the Author

Thelma Nurenberg has been an editor, journalist and lecturer, as well as the author of several books including the widely acclaimed novel *My Cousin, the Arab,* published by Abelard-Schuman, which created such comments from reviewers as: ". . . presents a frank and sometimes almost brutal picture of the building of Israel . . ." *(Booklist)*, ". . . It is a hard-hitting, realistic novel of people living in a world of hate and fear . . . the book renews that sense of wonder at the strength mankind possesses" *(Virginia Kirkus Service*—Special Mention), "This is Mrs. Nurenberg's first book for teen-agers—one hopes she will write many more. For her story is one that expands, that involves its readers in issues bigger than they, that shows the strength men possess" *(Christian Science Monitor).*

Mrs. Nurenberg's travels, to the Soviet Union, Europe, Scandinavia and Israel, are reflected in the authentic backgrounds of her books. When she isn't traveling, she is working at her typewriter in New York City.

About the Book

The text is set in Zenith.
The display type is Athenaeum.
Composed and bound by The Colonial Press Inc.